Nightmares Of a Hustla 3

**Lock Down Publications and Ca$h
Presents
NIGHTMARES OF A HUSTLA 3
A Novel by King Dream**

Lock Down Publications
P.O. Box 944
Stockbridge, Ga 30281

Visit our website @
www.lockdownpublications.com

Lock Down Publications
Like our page on Facebook: Lock Down Publications @
www.facebook.com/lockdownpublications.ldp

Book interior design by: **Shawn Walker**
Edited by**: Shamika Smith**

Stay Connected with Us!

Text **LOCKDOWN** to 22828 to stay up-to-date with new releases, sneak peaks, contests and more…
Thank you.

Submission Guideline.

Submit the first three chapters of your completed manuscript to ldpsubmissions@gmail.com, subject line: Your book's title. The manuscript must be in a .doc file and sent as an attachment. Document should be in Times New Roman, double spaced and in size 12 font. Also, provide your synopsis and full contact information. If sending multiple submissions, they must each be in a separate email.

Have a story but no way to send it electronically? You can still submit to LDP/Ca$h Presents. Send in the first three chapters, written or typed, of your completed manuscript to:

LDP: Submissions Dept
P.O. Box 944
Stockbridge, Ga 30281

DO NOT send original manuscript. Must be a duplicate.

Provide your synopsis and a cover letter containing your full contact information.

Thanks for considering LDP and Ca$h Presents.

King Dream

Chapter 1

The thundering sound of planes taking flight and landing on the tarmac pierced the Midwest summer air. Pay Pay and Noodles just landed in Milwaukee with their baby, Dayla, in hand. They stepped out of the Mitchell Airport and grabbed a rental car at the Enterprise Rental Company next door.

It's been almost a year since they took King Nut and his crew out of the game. Ever since then, Atlanta's been under the complete control of Pay Pay and the rest of The Order. Money was flowing like ocean water. But little known to him, trouble was brewing in other places.

Pay Pay got a call the night before from Billy Gunz. Billy Gunz told him to fly out to Milwaukee ASAP for an emergency meeting. The urgency in his voice conveyed the seriousness of the situation to Pay Pay, making him take the first flight out the next morning.

The luxury Mercedes Pay Pay rented entered into the gated community in the city of Mequon. As they drove through the gated community that rested on lake Michigan, they were in awe of their surroundings. Large, beautiful mansions with manicured lawns adorned the neighborhood with luxury cars parked in the long driveways. They pulled up to the gate of a mansion that sat close to the end of one block. Pay Pay pressed the button on the intercom to gain access. "Yes," a voice said from the other end of the intercom.

"Pay Pay and Noodles." A moment later, the huge iron gate with a gold letter B written in Old English font on the left side and the letter G was on the right side opened up. The Mercedes entered the premises and drove up the long and winding redbrick driveway. They parked behind a prune-colored Rolls Royce Wraith sitting on 24's.

"Daddy, is this Uncle Billy's and Aunt Missy's house?"

"Yeah, baby."

"Yayyy!" Dayla celebrated from her car seat in the back. She loved being around Billy Gunz, Missy, and their kids. They often came to Georgia to visit them, but this was her first time coming to their house and she was excited.

"Unfasten your seatbelt, babes and give me this candy," Noodles told her, taking the Hershey's bar out of her little hands. Noodles licked her finger and wiped the smeared chocolate off of Dayla's face.

"Ready?" Pay Pay asked her as she turned back around in her seat.

"Yeah, we're ready." At that, they got the car. Noodles grabbed Dayla out of the backseat and they approached the front door. The door swung open as they reached the top stair that led to the front door. An older, fat, white woman in a maid's uniform answered the door. After welcoming them into the house, she led them past the front entrance where a marble and gold statue of a lion and lioness sat on top of a cliff looking down on the lions below them. The grand staircase had pearl marble stairs and gold railings. They took the stairs to the second floor and walked down the hall, stopping at a pair of double doors on their left. Margaret, the maid, knocked on the door.

"Come in!" Billy Gunz's voice came from the other side. Margret opened the doors and they all walked into the meeting room-like office. Margaret leaves them be and closes the door behind her.

"Uncle Billy!" Dayla screamed with excitement as she ran into Billy Gunz's awaiting arms.

"There goes uncle's favorite niece!" He said as he scooped her up into his arms seconds before having her snatched away by Missy.

"Give me my sweet lil LaLa baby. Aunt Missy missed you so much," she said spoiling her chubby little cheeks with kisses.

After they all greeted each other Pay Pay and Noodles took a seat at the table. "Well, we're here. So, what's the word big homie?" Pay Pay asked. Billy Gunz peeled the skin off a green apple with a pocketknife.

"How you loving the next level of the game?"

"Let's see, we got a seat at the table as equal partners in The Order, we own a brand-new mansion now, four lucrative businesses, pushing almost thirty keys a week and our bank accounts are as fat as a hippo's ass. I can't complain, dog."

"You earned that and some. But I have to give yo' girl, Noodles, her credit for that move she and Paris pulled off. If it wasn't for her finding a way to get Giorgio out the way, we wouldn't have been able to secure our foothold on the Italians." He turned to Noodles. "And I see you were able to get a huge chunk of his tech company too. That was a boss ass move."

"Thank you."

"Okay, language is getting too heavy in here for the little one. Dayla, how would you like to go play with your cousins and eat some ice cream?"

"I like. I like!" She replied jumping up and down. Missy smiled at her.

"Noodles, want to help me make the girls some ice cream cones?"

"Yeah, let's go, I've been wanting to see the kids anyway." Noodles replied as she got up from her seat.

"Well, the boys are away at summer camp, but the twins will be excited to see the two of you." A few months after Dayla was born, Missy had given birth to Billy Gunz's twin girls.

"Okay. Well, let's go see aunt's twins," Noodles said as they left out the room. Pay Pay directed their attention back to the matter at hand.

"We appreciate the praise, big homie, but I doubt you called us all the way out here for a pat on the back. So, what's the deal, G? Why are we here?" Billy Gunz cut off a slice of the apple and ate it off the blade of the knife.

"We have a problem."

"What kind of problem?"

"A new crew of lil niggas that call themselves the No Love No Mercy clique, have been trying to take over streets out here. They've been robbing everybody's spots. Including our own."

"Lil niggas?"

"Yeah, lil niggas, from the ages of sixteen to twenty-two years old." Pay Pay chuckled.

"Is this some kind of joke or something?"

"I got enough money to buy Kevin Hart and many other comedians, you think I'd call you all the way out here to tickle my funny bone?" Pay Pay scratched the back of his head.

"I don't get it. If this is real talk, then why not just sic some of our soldiers on these niggas?"

"You think I ain't did that shit already? I tried that, but these lil niggas grow in numbers quicker than I can get rid of dey asses. If we don't do something pretty soon, they gonna outnumber us. I've been wrecking my brain trying to come up with a solution to this problem without making a mess that would draw too much attention to The Order."

"And I guess that's where we come in at." Billy Gunz sucked pieces of apple off his teeth.

"The two of you handled that last situation so well. What can I say? I admire y'all strategic approach to such matters. Just check out the situation and let me know how you suggest we go about this."

"Where these niggas be at?"

"You'll never guess." Billy Gunz cuts himself another slice of apple. "The east side." He eats the slice of apple off the blade. "Déjà vu, huh? They hang out by Truth's and Ticky's old stomping grounds. And they have a spot over there on the same block as Benny's bodegas. Their house shouldn't be hard for you to pick out." It was no doubt a feeling of déjà vu for Pay Pay. After the war with Truth and Ticky that spooked the whole city, he doubted anybody would have the balls to take over the east side, let alone the whole city. Now, once again, he might have to go to war with some niggas over that turf.

"Aight, I'ma check it out."

"You been gone from that type of shit for a couple years, lil bruh. Shit ain't what it used to be out there. So, my advice, stay low. At least until we can come up with a plan to best deal with the situation. Remember, you sit at the high table of The Order now, we can't afford any negative attention."

"Don't trip, I know somebody in the neighborhood that can set me up for a closer eye on them without drawing no attention to myself. I'ma peep the scene and get back with you."

"Cool, but in the meantime let's go have a lil fun."

King Dream

Chapter 2

Pay Pay looked out the window of the beautifully furnished up-stairs duplex on the east side of town. He then took a seat on the cushy Ashley furniture couch. "Terry I must say you really have been doing well for yourself." Terry walked into the room and handed Pay Pay a beer.

After all the drama and killing Ticky she checked herself into rehab and got her life together. She'd been clean ever since. She even went back to school to finish her nursing degree and became a registered nurse. She was a far cry from that dope fiend prostitute that she used to be. Even though she could never go back to the beauty she perfected before the drugs, she still looked good enough to turn heads.

"Yeah, and I couldn't do it without your help and support. I owe you big time. You've been a true blessing to me." She felt that she owed many thanks to Pay Pay for helping her get on her feet and get her life together.

"You don't owe me nothing." He twisted the top off the beer and took a swig from the bottle. "Now you said you got some info for me on those lil niggas across the street?"

"Yeah. Now you know I don't fuck around on the dope scene anymore, but I still know a few people who toot the horn. You remember Rick James?" She slid a coaster over to Pay Pay before he sat his beer down on her glass table.

"The one Ticky let the dogs eat up, right? That was a fucked-up way to go."

"Yeah, it was. But you know his whole family was crack addicts, from the mama on down. His lil sister, Bella, was the one everybody thought that was going to be something because she didn't get high. But when some nigga she was in love with and fucking with on the low left her ass, she started getting high. Then she found out she was pregnant with the nigga's baby and didn't even tell him. The bitch wouldn't even tell nobody who the father was. She named the baby Cîroc. You see that girl right there?" She points to a young woman sucking on a Bomb Pop. "That's Pumpkin. She's only twenty years old and she's out there bad. She mostly does powder and smoke primos, but every now and then she'll hit the pipe."

"That's a damn shame to be that young and out there like that. But why do I need to know about her?" Terry grabbed the half of the cigarette that sat in the ashtray and sparked it up.

"Because her boyfriend is Cîroc, the leader of the gang around here that calls themselves the No Love No Mercy Clique. They the ones that's been going around terrorizing the city and robbing all the dope boys' spots."

"You telling me these lil niggas across the street is the ones that's responsible for terrorizing the city and robbing my spots? I know my niggas out here ain't letting no lil niggas break them off and live to tell the story."

"You think anybody else would be dumb enough to go up against you and Billy Gunz? These lil niggas don't give a fuck about no one or nothing. They don't respect the laws of the streets or the Ol' G's. They think these streets belong to them. And if that don't convince you that they are the ones behind this shit, then check this out." Terry fiddles around on her phone for a second and then pulls up a video. "Pumpkin had loaded this video up on one of her social media pages. Cîroc made her take it down ASAP, but I was able to download it before she took it down. Check it out." She pressed play and the video began.

The video showed Pumpkin with a ski mask on, holding the phone selfie-style while filming. "Yeahhh, y'all know how us *No Love No Mercy* mothafuckas get down. We hit licks around this bitch, hoe," Pumpkin was boasting while smoking a blunt and blowing the smoke into the face of the camera. She showed three men behind her in ski masks holding guns. One of the men dumped a duffle bag full of bricks onto the table. The bricks were wrapped in gold plastic wrap with the symbol of The Order on them.

"Bitch, turn that mothafuckin camera off!" one of the men yelled at her.

"Damn nigga, you ain't gotta yell." She smacked her lips then the footage stopped.

"Was that enough to make a believer out of you?"

"I want all the info you can get me on these lil niggas. They don robbed the wrong niggas." She handed him a pair of binoculars.

"I got you. In the meantime, all you got to do is keep watching out that window and you'll see dey asses out there. That's their main spot right across the street there. Them dumb bastards be hanging outside all day and night. Right now, they at some party Pumpkin was telling me about. But they'll be back soon."

"And I'll be right here watching."

****

The next morning, Pay Pay checks the time on his Presidential Rolex. It wasn't even ten in the morning and the block was live. The young hustlas across the street ran up and down the block intimidating fiends to buy from them.

"Damn, these lil niggas don't sleep. Do they? At least they got that part of the game right," Pay Pay said to Terry while looking out the window with the binoculars.

"That's because of all of them damn Xannies, Percs and Mollies they be popping. Them lab rat fools can't sleep a lick. That's why dey ass so crazy now," Terry said as she ironed her clothes and watched her favorite soap opera on TV. Two flashy cars pulled up in front of the house he was watching across the street.

"Who is this nigga right here?"

"Let me see." She walks over and peeps out the window.

"The one getting out of that convertible BMW."

"Oh, that's Cîroc. He's the one who runs the No Love No Mercy clique. He calls all the shots."

"That lil nigga right there is the one calling all the shots?"

"Yup. He's like nineteen, but he's got a lot of clout around here. The one getting out that candy apple red Infiniti truck is his right-hand man, Wild-Child."

"You telling me Cowboy and the rest of these Ol' G's around here letting these lil hoe ass niggas run shit in the hood?"

"Shit ain't like it used to be, Pay Pay. When you, Billy, and em stopped showing y'all presence in the city like y'all used to, these lil niggas jumped off the porch. And they were so geeked up off the drugs, music, and shit they seen on TV, they started making their own rules to live by. And dem lil niggas are some ruthless mothafuckas. The damn police won't even patrol the block. The older niggas in the game are so scared of them, they don't even get in their way."

Pay Pay and Billy Gunz both stopped dealing with the minor dope deals and spots in the hood. They both were too busy running The Order and supplying the whole United States with weight. All the local dope deals fell on the laps of the cats they put in charge of the spots they had all around the city.

"Cowboy is actually letting this go on? I can't believe the shit I'm hearing." Cowboy is one of the Ol' G's Billy Gunz put in charge of the dope game on the east side of the city.

"Well, if you can't believe yo ears, then believe yo eyes. Because you see for yourself how they running this block. They just about got the whole city locked down like that."

A couple of the lil niggas unloaded some meat out of Ciroc's trunk and took it in the house. Two others grabbed bottles of liquor and two ice coolers out of Blow's trunk. Pay Pay zoomed the binoculars in on Cîroc and Blow as they conversed on the sidewalk in front of their house. "It looks like our lil friends are finna have themselves a party."

"That ain't nothing new. It's like a damn frat house over there. Every day they throwing some kind of party or get together. A bunch of lil hood rats running around there drunk, half-naked, and busting down with every nigga they see. Then once them niggas get all high and drunk, they get to shooting. Just doing a bunch of stupid shit." Terry shakes her head at the shame of it all. "You know my mama owned this duplex for years. She done seen a lot of shit go down over here. Including my daughter getting killed right on that very porch downstairs. And that still didn't make her leave this house. She was east side bound and loved this block. But when these lil bustards came around, it was too much for her to handle. She was too scared to even go outside to water her flowers because every time you turned around they were shooting."

"I see she moved somebody else in downstairs, so where she at?"

"She moved down to South Carolina with my aunts five months ago. I'ma tell you one thing though, you and Billy Gunz need to do something soon before these lil niggas fuck this whole damn city up," she said as she peeps out the blinds at them hanging out in front of the house across the street.

"Don't worry. I'm gon' take care of these lil niggas. I can promise you that."

King Dream

Chapter 3

The Rolls-Royce Wraith floated down I-94 like a cruise ship taking a voyage in the ocean. He bobbed his head as Scarface's song, Never, banged through the four twelves in the trunk. Maybach shades concealed his eyes from the bright summer sun. His arm rested on the opened window sill displaying his wrist that was wrapped in diamonds and his pinky ring that was just as icy. Talking with Pay Pay who sat in the passenger's seat and listening to his suggestions to their problem, Billy Gunz didn't feel any more confident in the problem being eradicated. He missed the days where he could lay a few head niggas of a clique down and the rest of the crew would bow down and respect his gangsta. But shit didn't work that way with these lil niggas. With them, you can cut the head off and another one more vicious grows right back. He lost more soldiers than he could count messing with those lil niggas. Something had to be done and Billy Gunz wasn't sure Pay Pay's plan was the right one.

His phone rang and he turned the radio down to answer it.

"Yeah."

"Billy G, this Cowboy."

"I know who it is. What's the business?"

"I just had a run-in with those No Love No Mercy cats. They ran up on me at the carwash with choppas out. Talking 'bout mothafuckas gon have to start paying a street tax to hustle out here. And they wanted to know who I was working for."

"And what did you tell em?"

"I told them I work for myself."

"And what they say then?"

"They wasn't buying that and demanded to meet with my boss. Told me that I had until tomorrow night to make it happen. Then them niggas robbed me."

"You telling me you let some lil niggas pop yo pockets and try to extort you?"

"You say that like it wasn't more of them than it was of me or if they wasn't standing there with a bunch of choppas in my face! It was nothing I could do, Billy. I was outnumbered and out-gunned." Billy Gunz exhaled a heavy breath.

"I know Cowboy. It's just these bastards is really starting to piss me off."

"What do you want me to do?"

"Setup the meeting for me with their boss."

"You sure you want to expose yourself to these niggas? They ain't really the diplomatic type."

"Just set it up. Tell him to meet me at the soccer field on Good Hope Road at 4:30 tomorrow evening."

"Whatever you say bruh." Billy Gunz ended the call. Pay Pay looked over at him.

"That sounded like mo problems."

"Nah, mo like they playing right into the hand of the plan," Billy Gunz said as he switched lanes and turned the music back up.

It's been a while since Billy Gunz let his presence be known in the streets. Being so high at the top of the game he had disassociated himself from the hood to keep the eyes of authorities off him. With hundreds of people working for him, it was no need to show his face. But now with everything that's been going on with the No Love No Mercy clique trying to take over the streets it was a must he showed his face. He had to ensure the real niggas in the city knew who the streets belong to.

He shifted the car into park in front of Love's Liquor Store. He spotted the last man he wanted to run into, but it was the one man he needed to see. The man was dressed in a blue Polo shirt with blue jeans shorts and a pair of Jordan's as he stood outside the store serving fiends. The man looked over at the Wraith that had just pulled up then turned his attention back to his hustle.

Billy Gunz stepped out of the car and walked towards the man. "If it ain't my nigga Cutthroat. Boy, I see ain't shit change. You back to hustling outside of yo' granddaddy's liquor store I see." The man didn't even look Billy Gunz way. He spit out a couple of rocks and served a hype that was standing in front of him.

Cutthroat, everybody called Cut for short, was Billy Gunz's right-hand man back in the day before The Order was established. He was also his half-brother on his daddy's side. A LeBron James looking-ass nigga. He got the name Cutthroat because he was so ruthless and felt no empathy for a mothafucka that crossed him or his peoples the wrong way.

"What you want Billy?"

"You don't sound too excited to see me. What, it's been seven or eight years since we last saw each other?"

"Try like twenty."

"It ain't been that long, has it?" Cut pulls out a loose cigarette from behind his ear and sparks it up. He blew out a cloud of smoke.

"I should know, I've done seventeen of those years in the joint for you. Then another three on probation and trying to get my life back together."

"You know I've been meaning to show my gratitude to you for that. I just been -" Cut held his hand up cutting Billy Gunz off.

"Save yo excuses, man. What is it you want?"

"Just cut to the chase, huh? Listen, I know you heard about these No Love No Mercy niggas trying to terrorize the city. They making shit real hard out here for hustlas like us to eat. I want you to help me get rid of these niggas so you can hustle in peace."

"Hustlas like us? Don't patronize me, Billy. Our hustle ain't on the same level and you know that. You all the way up there sitting on top of the mountain, top of heaven, getting yours and I'm down here in the valley of hell getting mine. Just look at you. You know you got some nerve, nigga, coming down here all jeweled up in your fancy Rolls-Royce and designer garments asking my po' black ass for some help. Besides doing yo time you couldn't even give me a spot in The Order when I got out. Instead, you have been keeping a distance from me like I got the COVID-19 virus or something. Acting like I don't even exist. Whose idea was it to start the order? Mines! All mines! And I couldn't even get a seat at the table. Instead, you put that soft ass nigga, K-Dolla, on the board along with this young punk you got riding shotgun with you looking out the window like some lapdog," he said pointing to Pay Pay sitting in the car. "The realest nigga you got on the team is Joey Long. That was the only nigga that tried to extend a helping hand my way while I was down and when I came home."

"You know why I couldn't reach out to you. I told you what was going on, Cut."

"And I told you I'm good on yo' excuses! You ain't slick nigga. You've become so used to these mothafuckas out here in the game bowing down to you and wiping yo ass every time you shit. Now that some trigger happy lil savages come along that don't give a fuck about the throne you sit on you need my help. But you come to me running this game like you doing me a favor by trying to get rid of these niggas. You came to me because YOU need ME," he expressed, pointing to Billy Gunz then at himself. "I don't need you, nigga. I'm a boss on my own. And I ain't worried about those No Love lil busters."

"You really going to grudge me out, bruh?" Cut mugged him up and down. Billy Gunz turned his head and sucked his teeth in frustration. Then he took off his shades and looked Cut in the eyes. "What you want? An apology?" Cut just looked at him. Fuck it, I was wrong Cut. I was wrong for abandoning you. But I'm not finna kiss yo' ass or beg you to forgive me. So just tell me what it is I can do to make this right between us?"

"Give me back all the years I lost fucking with yo' ass. When you can do that, then we can be good. Until then, go fuck yo' self, Billy!" Cut said as he took a hit of his square and blew the smoke out his nostrils. Billy Gunz put his shades back on and held his hands out to the side.

"To hell with you man. I tried, but you still the same ole stubborn bastard you was back in the day." Billy Gunz walked off to his side of the car and threw Cut some final words. "When you done rolling yo' eyes, smacking yo' lips, and acting like a hood rat on her period, give me a call."

With one hand holding the cigarette between his lips, Cut held up the middle finger on his other hand at him. Billy Gunz shook his head at him then got in the car and pulled off.

Pay Pay looked over at Billy Gunz, whose face he could tell was mugged up behind the tint of his designer shades. "That didn't seem to go too well."

"Skip that cry baby ass nigga."

"We can't just skip him, he's a major part of the plan."

"Well, we just gon have to change the plan a little then Pay Pay. Because I'm not finna kiss that stubborn bustard's ass!"

Cut wasn't the only one being stubborn Pay Pay thought.

Silence filled the car for several minutes before Pay Pay decided to speak again, "Let me ask you something?"

"How about you keep that question to yourself. Some questions shouldn't be answered. Some things are too complicated for the average understanding." He glanced over at Pay Pay. "You feel me?" Billy Gunz knew exactly what Pay Pay wanted to know. He wanted to know why he cut ties with Cut and what he did to go to the joint for. However, after hearing that, Pay Pay realized he wasn't going to get any answers to that question anytime soon.

"Yeah, I get what you saying."

"Cool. Now let's go get up with Cowboy and get on with the rest of the plan," he said as he cranked the music up, not so much as to hear the song, but to cut the conversation short so that he could sort out the thoughts in his head. And seeing Cut again brought many thoughts to mind to reminisce on. Thoughts of things he wished could've been left in the past. But he was starting to see that no matter how far you run from the past it still has a way of catching up to you.

Chapter 4

SWOOSH!! Was the swishing sound the bat made as it tore through the air and smashed square into Blaze's stomach. "Ahhh!" Blaze screamed as he doubled over in pain and spat out a small glob of blood.

They had been working him over for the past eight minutes and he didn't know how much more he could take. The man standing behind him holding his arms yanked him upwards to straighten him back up. Wild-Child swung the bat again, hitting Blaze in the leg that made him buckle and scream out in pain once again.

"Ooh, that gotta hurt. But let's see if I could do better than that. Let's go, Babe Ruth. Homerun, baby." He tapped the bat on the ground a few times before lifting back up in a batting position. "Batters up!" Before Wild-Child could swing his home run hit across Blaze's face, Cîroc held his hand up, stopping him.

"Let go of him," Cîroc told them. The man released his grip on him, and Blaze fell to his knees on the cold cement garage floor. Cîroc walked over to him and bent down to talk to him.

"Come on big Blaze, OG, you making this a lot harder than it should be. Now I know you got the plug on some heavy artillery. I need that plug. Also, I'm going to need you to reserve all sales of that heavy shit you got to only the No Love No Mercy clique." Blaze spit on the ground and chuckled.

"What I look like Boo Boo the fool to you? I ain't live this long, lil dog, from being stupid. What I look like giving you my plug?"

"Check it out, I ain't trying to eliminate you as the middleman. I know this here hustle is yo bread and butter and believe me when I say that I ain't trying to take too much food off your table. You can still sell those weak-ass Glocks and Nines or whatever to everybody else. What I'm telling you is to only sell the big shit to my clique and we're good. But if I hear you been selling Dracos, AKs, and shit like that to anybody outside my clique, I'm going to torture and kill all five of those lil crumb snatchers of yours while you watch. You get what I'm saying?" A knock on the garage door stopped Blaze from carrying out his first reaction of spitting in Ciroc's face.

"What!" Cîroc yelled at the door. The door opened and Lucci peeped in.

"Cîroc, Cowboy's here to see you."

"Let him in." Lucci stepped to the side and Cowboy walked in. He looked around the garage and saw Blaze on his knees beat up and Wild-Child holding a bloody bat. Knowing what Blaze's hustle was and Ciroc's constant need for guns, it wasn't hard for Cowboy to piece together the scene.

Blaze's been running guns since the early '90s. His plug was an old army buddy of his whose father owned a gun manufacturing company down in Texas. Blaze was able to get his hands on just about any type of heat a person needed, from two-shot Dillingers to weapons only seen on TV or in the hands of mercenaries. And he had no problem selling to anyone who had the cash to spend.

Putting two and two together, Cowboy knew Cîroc and his crew were trying to muscle Blaze into restricting his sale of guns to only people he approved of. Being the only ones with access to the best weapons gave them the greatest advantage in the game. It was their best move to be made if they were going to try and take over the whole city.

"You got two days, Blaze, to think on my proposal. See you in forty-eight hours to get yo answer," Cîroc told him. Blaze painfully got back up to his feet and limped out of the garage. "OG Cowboy. You got something good to tell me, ole head?" Cîroc said as he stood back up. Wild-Child stared at Cowboy while he wiped the blood off his bat with a dusty black T-shirt.

"I talked to my boss and he agreed to meet with you tomorrow. He said he'll be at the soccer field on Good Hope Road."

"And what time will I be meeting with the famous Ol' G Billy Gunz?" Cowboy gave him a look of shock.

"You look surprised. What, you didn't think I knew who it was you were working for? I know everything that goes on in these streets. Now, what times does he want to meet?"

"At 4:30." Cîroc walked up to Cowboy. He stood four inches shorter than Cowboy's six-foot frame, but still made Cowboy feel inferior to him.

"You tell Billy Gunz that I'll be there, and it'll be in his best interest not to try nothing slick. Because me and mine stay ready for whatever."

"I'll tell him. Anything else?"

"Nahhh, that'll be all." Cowboy straightened his cowboy hat on top of his head and slowly turned around hoping a bullet doesn't meet his back. The sound of the spurs on his cowboy boots rattling could be heard as he exited the garage.

"Who would ever think, a black cowboy in the hood. What kind of horse you think he galloped over here on?" Wild-Child said jokingly.

"That slug has been dressing like that since before we were born. I told you all these old heads is played out, style and all. That's why we're taking over the game. Lucci y'all niggas clean this shit up. Wild-Child let's ride up out of here."

****

Her caramel skin glistened with the shine of baby oil. Her short shorts showed off her juicy thighs. Her Gucci flip flops exposed her pretty feet and toes. And her shirt was small enough to show off her flat stomach, belly button piercing, and much of her cleavage. Her hair was braided into eight, long, red braids that ran down to the middle of her back. Her beautiful slanted brown eyes that always mesmerizes anyone she looked at, concentrated hard on the task she had at hand. She crossed her legs as she sat on her bed stuffing choirboy into her glass crack pipe. She dipped inside the bag of dope that set on the bed beside her and pulled out a fat dub size rock. Her nerves shook with anticipation as she loaded the rock into her pipe. The rock was so big she had to force it into the pipe causing some of the rock to come crumbling down the sides of the pipe. "Shit!" she said to herself as she brushed the crumbs off her shorts and into her hand. She placed the crumbs into the bag and sparked her pipe. The cherry amber inside the pipe glowed a bright fiery red and her jaws sunk in as she sucked hard on the pipe. In the middle of taking her first blast, someone knocked on her bedroom door. She sucked in a little more smoke and held it in a second. She made a sucking sound as she sucked the dope residue off her tongue. Another knock came on the door. "Who is it?" she asked as the smoke escaped her mouth as she spoke.

"Yo mama."

"What you want?"

"Open the door. I need to holla at you."

"We'll holla later, I'm busy right now."

"Nah, it's important. I need to holla at you now. Come on Pumpk-A-Pumpk, open the door." Pumpkin pursed her lips and narrowed her eyes at the door. Every time her mama called her Pumpk-A-Pumpk, she wanted something.

"Damn. Hold on." Pumpkin uncrossed her legs and got up off the bed. "Ugh, I swear to God that woman could smell dope being smoked on the moon. Every time I spark up her ass come a knocking right at my door," Pumpkin said to herself. She picked up the bag of dope off the bed and stuffed it in her bra. After getting herself together, she walked over to the door and undid the two deadbolt locks on her bedroom door. She put the locks on the door to keep the rest of the crackheads in the house from stealing her stuff.

She opened the door and Debbie pushed past her, walking over to the dresser.

"Okay, I see Cîroc bought you some new stuff." She picked up a bottle of cucumber Bath & Body Works body spray and sprayed some on as she talked. She saw a Victoria's Secret bag on the bed and pulled out a pair of hot pink boy shorts with a matching bra. "Ooh, this nice! You just got this? I'm going to need to borrow this." Pumpkin rolled her eyes and closed the door.

"I thought you wanted to talk to me not come in here shopping through my stuff."

"I do. But can I get a lil small talk in before I get to the heavy stuff?"

"Fine, you done had yo small talk now what? I got shit to do, ma."

"Let me get a hit right quick."

"You got some money?"

"Girl, you know I don't get my check until the first. Just let me get a hit off your horn." Pumpkin grabs the loaded crack pipe she hid under her pillow and gave it to Debbie.

"God damn, I can't have shit to myself in this house. Here!"

"Thank you, baby. Let me see yo lighter."

"What else, you want me to smoke it for you too?" She passed her the lighter. Debbie flicked the lighter and the flame shot up five inches in the air. The sizzling sound of the dope melting dominated the noise in the room as Debbie took a hard blast of the pipe. She held the smoke in then passed the pipe to Pumpkin. Pumpkin took a piece of wire hanger and pushed the dope down further into the pipe.

"Hey, I came in here cuz I needed to talk to you about the rent," Debbie said as she blew out the cloud of dope smoke that filled her lungs. She sat there on the edge of the bed next to Pumpkin staring off into space. The blast she took activated fast and had her stuck.

"What about it?" Debbie turned to her with puppy dog eyes.

"I'm a little short."

"What? How you short and I just gave you some money for rent the other day?"

"I know, but I had owed Bay Bay fifty dollars for some dope I had got on credit last week. And can you believe he's been hounding me like crazy for that lil money? So, I had to hit his hand to get him off my ass and now I'm short."

"Wow, unbelievable." Pumpkin turned her back to her mama and reached inside her bra and pulled out a fat knot of money. She peeled off a fifty and handed it over her shoulder to her mama.

"I appreciate this and don't mean to be a burden baby, but I'm actually short a hundred dollars now."

"What? How is you short a hundred when you only borrowed fifty?"

"Because when I got there, he had some new dope he was pushing off on me. And I ended up having him spot me another fifty. I'm sorry, Pumpkin."

"I don't understand. Why don't you just cop yo' work from me?"

"Now baby, you know I don't mix family and business. So, I got to get mines how I can." It took everything in Pumpkin to bite her tongue and not curse her mama out. So instead of giving her a piece of her mind and risking an argument or fight, she just peeled off another fifty along with a dub of crack and handed it to her.

"Make sure the landlord gets that. And from now on I'll deliver the rent to him myself. Fucking with you we'll be on the streets smoking out of cardboard boxes." Debbie's face lit up. She wasn't paying any attention to what Pumpkin was saying. All she cared about was that she got what she wanted. She kissed Pumpkin on the forehead.

"Thank you, baby. That's mama's Pumpk-A-Pumpk right there. Girl, I don't know what I would do without you, you hear me?" Debbie said as she stuffed the money in her bra then left out the room.

Pumpkin knew her mama was just running game on her. She was used to her doing things like that and playing on her emotions to hustle up her next high. One time when Pumpkin was fourteen, Debbie went even as far as to beat herself up with an orange inside a sock. After the bruises appeared, she told Pumpkin a drug dealer she owed money to did it to her. She had explained that if she didn't pay him two-hundred dollars soon, he was going to kill her. Fearing for her mother's life, Pumpkin went out and hit her first lick. She robbed a gas station with a toy gun and got five-hundred and sixty-seven dollars out of the cashier. Little amount out the gate, but though she knew it was just the beginning of being a hustla and her mother's keeper. That same day her mama introduced her to smoking crack. Ever since that day she's been hitting licks and hustling to keep them both high and getting by.

Her phone chimed. She looked down at it and saw that it was a text message from Cîroc. The text read:

Come over 2morrow nite for a lollipop...

It was their code for having a sweet lick to hit. Pumpkin texted back, Okay, then tossed the phone on the bed.

She grabbed her pipe and loaded it back up. Ready to take her blast, she searches for her lighter. She couldn't find it. Then it dawned on her. "Her ass got me for my lighter!"

King Dream

Chapter 5

The stands were sprinkled with half masked people watching the game while keeping their respective distance due to the Covid-19 virus. The soccer players were drenched in sweat as they ran up and down the field playing their hearts out.

The team wearing green and white scored a goal. Billy Gunz stood up, pulled his Versace face mask down and put his fingers in his mouth to whistle. He clapped his hands and pulled his mask back over his mouth and nose. Just as he did so Cîroc showed up with Wild-Child and Pumpkin by his side. They spotted Billy Gunz in the stands and made their way over to him.

"There he is y'all, the legendary Billy Gunz himself. I knew if I made enough noise out here in these streets you come out of hiding to see me. You mean to tell me that you're so much a bad ass that you came out here all by yourself?" Cîroc said as he took a seat next to him. Wild-Child and Pumpkin took a seat behind Billy Gunz and Cîroc.

Billy Gunz ran his tongue across his gold teeth and made a sucking sound. "To bring someone along with me would mean I feel threatened in your presence." Billy Gunz took his eyes off the game for a brief second and looked Cîroc and his crew up and down. "And around y'all, I feel safer than a kitten fighting a toothless dog."

"This nigga can't be too smart. If you feel that safe fool, I can prove you wrong. I mean, what's really stopping me from popping yo' top off right now?" Wild-Child asked as he raised his shirt up a little and exposed his 9mm Ruger to Billy Gunz. Billy Gunz looked at the steel Wild-Child clutched on his waist and chuckled at his ignorance.

"Hopefully common sense and observation. Look around you, chump." Wild-Child and the rest of the team looked around the field and saw a sign that said Midwest Law Enforcement Soccer League Game.

"The team in the yellow and white is law enforcement officials from Indiana. And the ones in the green and white are from here. This whole field and stands are filled with DA's, police, FBI, judges, and other forms of law enforcement. I can guarantee you they all are packing. You shoot me, none of y'all asses will walk out of here alive. So, we either get to dying or cut the bullshit and let's talk business." Wild-Child flipped his shirt back down over his pistol. "Smart move. But next time you should try being more aware of your surroundings," Billy Gunz told him before putting his eyes back on the game.

"You wanted to meet with me, young dog. Well, here I am. Say what's on yo' mind. But be quick because my time is valuable," he told Cîroc as he raised his arm and check the time on his Rolex.

"Growing up my big cuz used to tell me these wild gangsta stories about you, and I can't lie. I admired your gangsta all my life. At one point, I even wanted to be just like you. That was until I learned I can be better than you. You've been ruling these streets for a long time, old-timer."

"That's nice to know I'm your ghetto hero, but I would really like for you to get to the point of this story," Cîroc smirked at Billy Gunz's arrogance.

"My point is: this is a new age and you and your team are too washed up to get with the program. So out of respect for you, I called this meeting to let you know it's time for you to retire. Now, I don't know if you notice or not, but these streets are mine now." The green and white team stole the ball from the other team.

"Let's go, Baby!" Billy Gunz yelled and clapped his hands. "You sound so confident in succeeding in taking these streets from me."

"Because I got enough muscle and balls to do so."

"You assume so. But let's say your assumption is right. You still lack the brains needed to succeed in doing so." Billy Gunz chuckled. "You young dumb chumps kill me. Y'all gangsta and no sense. Y'all priorities are all fucked up. You want to take over the streets but ain't got the dope plug to do so. You can't keep robbing potential clientele for their work to stay in business."

Pumpkin tried to stay on point with what was going on, but she was too high to stay focused. She couldn't sit still, and Billy Gunz took notice of her condition. "Yo girl alright over there? She's acting all fidgety. She looks like she's in need of a blast." Cîroc looked over at her as she tried her best not to look high.

Cîroc didn't know she got high, and she tried her best to keep him in the dark about it. She was in love with Cîroc and afraid if he found out about her little habit, he would leave her. She wanted to quit, but her habit was too heavy to shake. With her eyebrows furrowed, she confronts Billy Gunz's comment.

"I don't get high! I just ain't comfortable being around all these damn police," she said looking around at all the law enforcement. Her reply was enough said to satisfy Cîroc, so he ignored the whole thing and continued the conversation with Billy Gunz where they had left off.

"I got a plug. In fact, I got *thee* plug."

"Who?"

"You."

"You trying to muscle the streets from me and get me to supply you. And let me guess, you expect me to sell to you and only you too, right?"

"You catching on, ole timer."

"Boy, you got to be dumber than a valley blonde if you believe for one second that's gon' happen. What would ever make you think I would do something as retarded as that?"

"Because I know things about you that other people don't. Things that you wouldn't want certain people to find out."

"You don't know shit about me, lil dog. Because if you did, my very presence alone would have you scared enough to shit your pants," Billy Gunz told him as he stared coldly into his eyes. Cîroc studied the ominous look in his eyes a moment. Then he broke eye contact and produced a fake shiver.

"Ooh, spooky. Throughout my life, I heard a lot of scary stories about you. But I guess I always been kind of fucked up in the head because the scarier the story the more I wanted to come for you." Cîroc paused a moment to light his cigarette. "My favorite story of all though was the one about you and what went down in Corpus Christi, Texas with the Bread-Man." Billy Gunz's heart almost stopped when he heard what he said. Cîroc saw the look of shock that quickly riddled Billy Gunz's face. That look on his face made Cîroc smirk with confidence. He knew he had a well-played move that would get him exactly what he wanted. "You a cold-hearted mothafucka for that one, BG."

"I don't know what you're talking about."

"Sure, you do. And I know somebody that's dying to know what really went down there. I'll give you a couple of days to think things over. I'm sure if you want your lil secret to remain what it is, then we'll be doing business together real soon." Billy Gunz snatched him by the arm. Pumpkin and Wild-Child started to make a move on Billy Gunz, but Cîroc held a hand up stopping them.

"I don't give a damn what you think you know, but I'll never bow down to your demands." Cîroc stood up and straightened his clothes and chuckled.

"We'll see about that. But as the French say, ta-ta for now." He chucked Billy Gunz the deuces and motioned his head for Wild-Child and Pumpkin to ride out.

Billy Gunz's eyes followed them as they left the stands. He could've put a bullet in the back of his head. He couldn't believe Cîroc could possibly know anything about what happened in Corpus Christi. All of that went down well before Cîroc was even born. He had to find out how he knew about that situation. Because whoever told him was another person that was a must that he eliminated ASAP.

King Dream

Chapter 6

Varieties of exotic foods adorned the table. A fountain of champagne overflowed the champagne flutes stacked into the form of a pyramid on the table. Guests dressed in tuxedos and evening gowns danced on the backyard dance floor. The famous sax player Kenny G entertained the prestigious guests in Billy Gunz's backyard with the sweet melodies of his saxophone.

Billy Gunz sat at his table staring off into space. Missy looked over at him and nudged him back down to earth. "What?"

"You tell me. We got the mayor, the governor, and every elite class of individual in Wisconsin here in our backyard for you to woo and you're just sitting here staring off into space. I know you're not second-guessing your business plan, are you?"

"Of course, not "

"Great because you shouldn't, it's a good plan."

"I just can't get something Cîroc said out of my head ."

"About you retiring from the streets? You've been in the dope game long enough, baby, and we got enough money now to secure eight generations of wealthy living. If you ask me, it's no better time than now for you to make your exit out of the game. I mean, isn't that the whole reason you're trying to woo these guests into investing in your business plan? So, you can go all the way legit?"

"Yeah, it is. But I'm not going to leave the game in the hands of that young punk. I ain't work this hard making the game what it is for the kingdom to fall into the wrong hands. Anyways, that ain't what's bothering me."

"Then what is?"

"He knows about Corpus Christi."

"What!"

"Keep your voice down," Missy spoke so loud, a group of guests looked over at them. She quickly plastered a fictitious smile on her face.

"I thought you said he's nineteen years old. How the hell could he possibly know about Corpus Christi?" she whispered to him.

"I don't know. But what I do know is we need to find out more about this kid and who he really is, or things going to get real ugly real quick." A look of worry grew on Missy's face. A backyard full of guests was the only thing keeping her from expressing the full extent of the panic she felt. But Billy Gunz knew exactly what she was feeling. He put his arm around her shoulder and whispered in her ear.

"We gon fix this. But for now, let's get these business investments," he told her as he stood up from his seat and buttoned the button on his tuxedo jacket, and walked off.

****

The rhythmic sound of the headboard banging against the wall and the bed springs squeaking gave melody to their lovemaking. Sweat ran down the path between her breast and dipped down into her belly button as she rode him. His hands squeezed her rear as they guided the rhythm of her hips.

"Ooh, Cîroc!" Pumpkin moaned as she came closer to her passion. She tilted her head back and let out a cry of pleasure as she made it to her destination. She fell over on top of him breathing hard but still grinding on him so he can get his.

"You ain't got to keep going, I'm good."

"But you ain't get yours."

"Because I ain't want to. This session was all about pleasuring you, baby." He kissed her lips.

"You sure? Because I can go down there and do that thing you like if you want," she said as she started to make her way down his body. He stopped her and pulled her back up.

"I'm sure. Gon' in there and jump in the shower. I'm going to join you in a minute."

"Okay, baby," she said as she gave him a kiss and got to her feet. He watched as her hips swayed from side to side as she exited the room and into the bathroom across the hall. She closed the door behind her and a few moments later he could hear the sound of the shower running. He jumped up out of bed and went straight for her stuff.

Lately, he had been having a feeling that she might have been using. The buck red eyes, paranoia, rapid speech, and constant movement were a dead giveaway for him. When he first noticed it, he questioned her about it. She swore up and down he was tripping, and she wasn't using. She even made him feel bad for even asking her such a question. And for a minute, he thought that maybe he was tripping. But when Billy Gunz noticed it too, he knew it had to be something to it.

He rummaged through her pants pockets but found nothing but a couple hundred dollars and a hair scrunchy. He throws her jeans back on the floor and goes for her purse. He unzipped it but finds nothing more than a pack of Newport, some White Owl cigars, lip gloss, makeup, and a bag of Skittles. He thought for sure he was going to find a crack pipe or some type of dope fiend paraphernalia in her stuff. He zipped the purse up and sat it back down then let out a breath of relief.

His phone rang. He crawled across the bed and picked his jeans up off the floor. He dug his phone out and checked the caller ID then answered it. "What up big cuz?" He answered as he sat down on the bed.

"What's happening? How's things going on yo end?" Cîroc leaned over and peeped out the door before replying.

"Everything's going as planned. I wish you could've seen the look on Billy Gunz's face when I mentioned I knew all about Corpus Christi, Texas, and the Bread-Man. He was so frightened his heart could've jumped out his chest." Cîroc chuckled at the memory of it all.

"I bet he was. Did you give him our demands?"

"I told him I'm running things now and he's not allowed to serve no one but me. And I told him he had two days to make a decision or I'm going to make it for him."

"Spoken like a true boss."

"No doubt. But he wasn't folding; he said he didn't care what I knew he wasn't given in. So, what now?"

"Knowing Billy Gunz and how he operates, he's trying to find out everything he can about you. He wants to know how you know about Corpus Christi. Then he's coming to cut all loose ends. And when he comes, we'll make our move. So, for now, stay on yo toes and keep playing the game like I told you. When all is said and done, we'll have everything we need lil cuz. Be smooth. I'll holla at you later. Peace."

"Peace." Cîroc disconnects the call and with a grin on his face, he gets up and heads to the bathroom to join Pumpkin in the shower.

****

Drool slid down the head of a freshly baked gingerbread man as Dayla took a bite of the warm cookie. Crumbs and drool fell on the couch as she sat between her grandmother's legs chewing her cookie. Pay Pay and Noodles sat next to each other as they looked through Pay Pay's family photo albums.

"Oh my god! Mama Resa I can't believe you still have this photo!" Noodles said as she looked at a photo of Pay Pay, her, Baby Red and Do-Dirty posing in front of Ol' G Poky's Deuce and a Quarter.

"Yeah, sad for me mama don't throw away nothing that would embarrass me."

"And why would I? It's one of the perks of being a mother." Resa said as she plaited Dayla's hair.

"Look at you with a Wave Nouveau in yo' head." Noodles pointed to the picture and laughed.

"I know you ain't laughing. Look at you with them old ass B-Boots and baggy ass Guess jeans on," Pay Pay said pointing at her wardrobe in the picture.

"I don't know what you talking about, that was fly back then and you know it."

"Yeah, yeah, yeah," Pay Pay said, reaching over and turning the page.

"Whoa, who's the handsome stud in the suit?" Noodles pointed to a picture of a man in a pinstriped suit standing outside a country club in Texas. His hand rested on the shoulder of a teenage boy with a sly smile on his face.

"That was my pops."

"Dayum, I almost thought that was you. Y'all look just alike. You never told me much about him."

"It's not much to tell. He was a big-time business analysis who was always gone on business trips and rarely had any free time. He died in a car accident when I was about five or six. So, it's not much I really remember about him." Pay Pay pulled the photo album closer to get a better look at the picture. "That's funny, I don't ever recall seeing this picture of him before."

"Let me see." Resa leaned over her from her side of the couch towards their way to get a look at the picture. "That was taken the night before he passed."

"Who's the boy standing beside him?" Resa smiled at the photo.

"That's your cousin Martin."

"My cousin? I ain't never met him. To be honest, now that I think about it, I never met anyone on pop's side of the family. What's up with that?"

"That's because they live down in San Antonio, Texas. Martin is your father's sister, Edna's, son. The only decent person I could say on that side of your family. And that boy loved yo daddy. Every time Bobby would come down there, Martin would follow him everywhere he went."

"So why y'all never took me down there to meet that part of my family?"

"The truth is that side of your family wasn't too fond of me or you. And I didn't want you going down there being around all those snooty snobs with their noses all up in the air at you because you're my son."

"And why don't they like us?"

"Because us and them are from two different worlds. And they are the type of people that feel those worlds should never meet. They told me I was a poor nappy head girl from the ghetto that just wanted to use your father for his money. And when I had you, they disowned your dad and cut him off and didn't want anything to do with you."

"Well, I'm glad you didn't force me to be around them people. But I'm curious as to how did that side of the family make their fortune?"

"Like most Texans do, oil. Your great grandaddy had found oil on his property and made millions and paved the way for the success of his descendants."

"To be black, handsome, and rich, you must've had to fight them girls off his daddy with a stick, Mama Resa," Noodles said and made Resa laugh.

"More than you know. Let me tell you about this one time I caught this girl at my job trying to make her move on him." As Resa began telling her the story, Pay Pay zoned out.

He stared at the picture of his dad and Martin, and he couldn't help but get a familiar feeling when he looked at Martin. It felt like he'd seen him before somewhere. Pay Pay tried his best to dredge up memories of his father hoping it could explain that familiar feeling he kept getting about Martin. As hard as he tried nothing came to mind. But the feeling was so strong it was irritating him that he couldn't figure it out. His gut told him it was something he had to dig further into, and that he was.

King Dream

Chapter 7

K-Dolla and his wife, Victoria, slid into the awaiting limousine as they left the New Life Baptist Church in Milwaukee where he was paid five thousand dollars to appear as a special guest preacher. He figured if he had to come out there for a meeting that Billy Gunz had called, he might as well get paid while he was there.

K-Dolla leaned back in his seat with his head to the ceiling and loosened his tie. Victoria poured him a drink of Scotch on the rocks and herself a glass of Ace of Spades. "Here you go, my love. What's wrong? You're looking tense." She passed him his drink with a look of worry on her face.

"Thanks, baby." He took a swig and let out an 'ah' sound as the warm liquor slid down his throat. "I got a bad feeling about this meeting with Billy tomorrow. He sounded strange on the phone. In all the years I've known him, I've never heard him sound so worried. And if something was bad enough to put him on edge, then I know I most definitely should be worried." Victoria rubbed a gentle hand through his hair.

"Did he give you a hint of what this could be about?"

"All he said was that it's some bad news from the past."

"You don't--" She stopped in mid-sentence when she noticed the limo driver looking at them through the rearview mirror and eavesdropping. She reached over and pressed the button raising the partition. She lowered her voice when she began to speak again. "You don't think it has anything to do with the Bread-Man, do you?"

"It couldn't. No one outside of you, me, Missy, Cutthroat, Joey Long, Billy Gunz, and the Bread-Man knows about what went down in Corpus Christi. And the Bread-Man isn't alive to tell." K-Dolla took a big gulp of his drink. The thought of that being a possibility made him nervous.

"I don't know. Like you said, it's probably nothing." He reached over and poured himself another drink to calm his nerves.

Victoria stared out the window of the limo as her mind reflects back to the events that led up to that fateful day in Corpus Christi...

A rolled-up beach towel supported Victoria's head as she laid stretched out on the deck of an expensive, luxurious yacht. Her black two-piece Dior bikini showed off her flawless body. She protected her eyes from the sun's rays with a pair of Chanel sunglasses. Her brown skin shined and tanned in the blazing sun. With the waves rocking the boat back and forward, it made her feel like she could fall asleep right there. But as relaxed as she felt, falling asleep was something she couldn't do. She felt the molesting eyes of Carlito lusting over her half-naked body.

It was Carlito's yacht she and her father were sailing in. Carlito was her father's boss and the kingpin of Colombia. Carlito was a man who got whatever he wanted by any means it took to get it. But it was one thing he wanted he could never get and that was Victoria. He tempted her with money and extravagant gifts, but Victoria gave no interest to him. It was someone who had her heart and she couldn't wait until they dock so she could see him.

The yacht sailed the Caribbean Sea from Barranquilla Colombia to Corpus Christi, Texas where it docked. A limousine and two Lincoln Town Cars met them at the dock. The limousine driver stepped out and opened the rear passenger's door and out came the tall muscular man they called the Bread-Man. Carlito and the Bread-Man met halfway up the walkway and embraced in a hug.

Victoria and her father, Javier, stopped beside one of the town cars. "Victoria, as usual, I'll meet you back at the hotel. Kevin here will take you anywhere else you need to go." Javier leaned in closer and whispered in her ear, "Remember, I'm counting on you."

"You know I won't disappoint you, daddy." She kissed her father on the cheek and got in the backseat of the car. Kevin, AKA K-Dolla, one of the Bread-Man's men, closed the door behind her then turned and faced Javier. Javier put a hand on K-Dolla's shoulder.

"Kevin you make sure you look after my little girl. Your life does depend on it. You got me?"

"Yes sir. Just as usual she's in good hands, Javier."

"Good." Javier pats him on the back and walks off. Javier along with Carlito got into the limousine with the Bread-Man.

As soon as the limo drove off with the other town car behind it, Victoria climbed between the two front seats and wrapped her arms around K-Dolla then pressed her lips against his. K-Dolla pushed her off him.

"Damn baby, slow down. At least wait until the limo is out of eye shot. Your daddy see us together he'll kill me."

"Don't be such a scary cat. My father is more focused on the business that's being discussed in the back of that limo than what could be going on between you and me."

"I doubt that. You don't see the way he looks at me. I swear Victoria, it's like he knows it's something going on between us." Victoria leaned in and kissed him again and caressed his earlobe with her mouth.

"Are you going to spend the little time we got together worrying about what my father might or might not know about us? Or are we going to go somewhere and have some fun?" With nothing further to be said K-Dolla put the car in drive and drove off.

After getting hot in the backseat of the car, they spent the evening shopping and catching a movie along with dinner before he took her back to her hotel suite. He walked her to her room door.

She slipped the key card out of her purse and into the door unlocking it. He made sure no one was watching and gave her a quick kiss.

"Goodnight, Victoria." He turned to leave. She grabbed him by the arm.

"Where you going?"

"Home."

"Why? My father called while we were out and said they wouldn't be back until late tonight. They're gonna party a little bit. You know how they do when we come to the States. Come inside and keep me company."

He thought about it a second. He knew he was already playing with fire by fooling around with Javier's daughter and everything in him was telling him it would be a bad idea to go in. But the power of list and love defeated any resistance he had. He looked around then walked inside the room and the two began to fulfill their lustful desires.

An hour and a half later they both lay covered in sweat. He got up and put his boxers on and walked into the bathroom to take a piss and a quick wash up. A smiling Victoria sits up in bed and lights up a joint.

Minutes later the toilet flushed and K-Dolla walked out of the bathroom. His heart could've stopped when he saw who was waiting in the room for him. Javier stood in the room with a gun in each hand. Though they weren't pointed at him the threat still felt the same. He put his hands up. "Javier, it's not what it looks like." Victoria sat with her back against the headboard and her knees close to her chest clutching the sheets over her naked body. He could tell she was just as scared as him of what her father might do to him.

"You saying you're not standing here in my hotel room with my nude daughter wearing nothing but your underwear?" K-Dolla

was at a loss for words. It was no lie he could've told that would manipulate the situation to look any different from what was really going on.

"Papi, I can explain." Javier shot her a stern look that instantly silenced her. She put her head down in shame and he steered his focus back on K-Dolla.

"You think my daughter is some whore to lay when you get a prick in your pants? Or are you getting off on the fact you can fuck the daughter of a man as powerful as me?" He raised his guns and pointed them at K-Dolla while walking towards him.

The room temperature was warm but K-Dolla still shook. Powerful currents of fear shot through his body making it hard for him to stand. By the time Javier got across the room to him, he had fallen to his knees begging for mercy at his feet.

"Javier, I swear it's nothing like that! I'm in love with your daughter. Please don't kill me!" Tears fell from his eyes as he begged. Javier pressed the barrel of one of the guns to the top of his head.

"You love her? I should kill you right now for deflowering my sweet little girl!" Spit shot from his mouth and fell on the back of K-Dolla's head as he yelled. He cocked back the other gun and pressed it hard against K-Dolla's head.

"Daddy, no!!" K-Dolla was sure it was his end. He was so scared he threw up. Some of the vomit splattered onto Javier's alligator cowboy boots and made him take a couple of steps back.

"Victoria, you love this man?"

"Yes, Papi!"

"Look at him. He can't even face death like a man without puking and crying like a baby." Javier bent down and pointed one of the guns in his face. "Look me in the eyes like a man and tell me you love my daughter." Coughing with tears and spittle running

down his face K-Dolla slowly raised his head and looked Javier in the eyes.

"I Love her." He then looked over at Victoria. "I love you Victoria and want to marry you." Javier's eyes narrowed as he read him.

"I believe you may love her. But let's see how much you love her. I have a proposition for you. If you accept it, I won't only give you my daughter's hand in marriage, but I will also make you a very rich man." K-Dolla wiped his mouth off with the back of his hand and got back to his feet. At the same time, Javier stood back up.

"What's the proposition?" Javier shook his head and waved his finger at him.

"No, no, no. You won't know the proposition until you agree to it."

"You want me to agree to something blindly?"

"Exactly! There's too much at stake. If I tell you and you don't agree to it, I will have to kill you. To save a bullet or two and my daughter any heartache, you would have to agree to do this before I tell you what it is that I want you to do. Besides, if you truly love Victoria, then isn't she worth doing whatever for?" K-Dolla looked over at Victoria. Her beautiful wavy black hair flowed down her shiny unblemished brown skin. Her big brown eyes were saddened into a puppy dog look. He knew he would do whatever it took to have her forever. And to get rich in the midst was just a cherry on top. He looked back at Javier.

"I'll do it." Javier returned his guns to their holsters then slapped a hand on K-Dolla's shoulder.

"Now you sound like a man who deserves my daughter. Get dressed and let's talk." As K-Dolla walked away, Javier looked at Victoria and winked his eye at her and she shot back a sly smile. And just like that, the perfect storm was taking motion.

Victoria snapped back to reality from her trip down memory lane. She looked over at K-Dolla and saw that he had fallen asleep. She looked out the window and got a strange feeling. She elbowed K-Dolla waking him up. "Yeah, what?" His eyes were still closed when he spoke to her.

"Wake up! This isn't the way to the hotel."

"Maybe the driver's taking another route. Wake me up when we get there." Still not wanting to open his eyes he turned to his side and leaned against the door and tried to go back to sleep. She elbowed him harder.

"Get Up! There's no dirt road route to the hotel. Now get up and do something!" Reluctantly, he woke up. He wiped his eyes then looked out the window. His eyes grew big looking out the window at nothing but rural land and woods. He reached over and pressed the button and opened the partition.

"Driver, are you lost? Where are we? This is not the way to our destination." The driver gave him a cold stare through the rearview mirror then raised the partition back up. "What the -" K-Dolla pressed the button again and again but the partition wouldn't come back down. Then came a clicking sound and the door locks engaged.

"Honey, what's going on?" Victoria asked as she tried to open the door, but it wouldn't budge. Childproof-like locks kept the doors from opening from the inside. She tried the windows with no luck. They were trapped inside. They tried their phones but there was no signal. Trapped inside the limo with no weapons or any way to call for help, Victoria and K-Dolla were as good as dead.

King Dream

Chapter 8

Billy Gunz followed Cîroc to a Walgreens on 45th and North Avenue. Billy Gunz parked in front of a store that sat kitty-corner to the Walgreens parking lot. Incognito in a dope fiend rental minivan, he watched as Cîroc and Pumpkin got out of the car and hugged. Cîroc held up his phone and said something to her. She nodded her head and walked off down the block. Cîroc walked into the Walgreens then came out a few minutes later and got back in his car and drove away. Billy Gunz got ready to follow him but stopped when something caught his eye. He pulled his shades off thinking maybe his eyes were playing tricks on him. He watched as Pumpkin ran into the open arms of another man. A man to whom he knew all too well. Pumpkin and Cutthroat disappeared into the upstairs residence of a green and white duplex. "I guess now I know how Cîroc found out about Corpus Christi."

Thirty minutes later Pumpkin came out of the house and walked to the corner store where Billy Gunz was parked. She walked right past his car and right into the store not knowing she just passed him.

"Cut and I may not be seeing eye to eye right now, but this shit he doing with Cîroc and that bitch is crossing the line. I'm going have to remind his shady ass who the fuck he's messing with, as soon as I take care of Cîroc and his girl." He tightened his face mask and put his hood over his head. Checked the ammunition in his clip then slipped the clip back in and jumped out of the van leaving the sliding backdoor open.

He crouched behind a dumpster next to the store. Three minutes later Pumpkin came strolling out the store with a small brown paper bag in one hand and a Tahitian Treat soda in the other. Billy Gunz came from out of his hiding place as she reached the curb.

She looked both ways as she readied herself to cross the busy intersection. Before she could take another step, Billy Gunz had slammed the butt of his gun in the back of her head. She didn't have time to figure out what had happened before her eyes rolled into the back of her head and she lost consciousness. Billy Gunz caught her before she hit the ground and dragged her into the backseat of the minivan then slid the door shut. He looked around for any witnesses. Satisfied no one had seen what he just did, he calmly walked over to the driver's side and casually drove off.

Billy Gunz pulled the minivan into the garage of one of Cowboy's spots on the east side. He got out of the van and slid open the side door. Pumpkin was still knocked out. He put her over his shoulder and carried her into the house.

Cowboy was sitting in his Lazy Boy chair watching the Green Bay Packers play the Dallas Cowboys on the television when Billy Gunz came through the door. The sound of the screen door slamming close made Cowboy take his eyes off the television and look towards the door. "What you got there, Billy G?" He pointed to the woman across his shoulders. "I never took you for the caveman type when it came to the ladies." Cowboy joked.

"This here is collateral, and I need it kept locked away safe in the basement."

"You know where it is." He turned his bottle of beer up in the air and chugged it. Billy Gunz locked the front door. When he came closer into view Cowboy got a look at the woman across his shoulders. When he saw her his eyes almost jumped out their sockets and he spat out his beer. "You got to be shitting me. That's Ciroc's bitch!"

"I know who she is."

"Then you got to know them lil boys' spot is up the street from here." Billy Gunz walked past him. Cowboy followed him into the basement.

"Her and Cîroc were trying to make a major play on us, and we got to nip that shit in the bud. You feel me?"

"You kidnapped his bitch, what now? You can't keep this dope head broad here forever." Billy Gunz laid her on a cot in a window-less room in the basement with a toilet and sink. He snapped a photo of her with her phone then closed the door behind him. He held out his hand to Cowboy. Cowboy dug into his pocket and produced a set of keys. He went through the ring of keys until he found the one, he was searching for then handed it to Billy Gunz. Billy Gunz used the key to lock the two deadbolt locks on the door one by one. One deadbolt at the top and one where a doorknob should've been. He gave the door a push to make sure it was locked tight.

"She gets high, huh? I figured she was a smoker."

"She used to get her high from me to keep Cîroc from finding out she smoked. But answer my question. What are we going to do with her? That boy loves this clucked-out bitch. He's going to tear these damn streets up looking for her.

"Don't worry about it, I got a plan. I stripped her of her phone and everything else and that door is made of steel, she ain't going nowhere and no one's going to find her. You just keep an eye on her while I put some more moves in play. Alright?"

"You the boss." Billy Gunz handed him back the keys then shook his hand and gave him a manly embrace.

Billy Gunz left out the house and jumped into the minivan. He went back to the south side to drop the minivan back off to the hype then caught an Uber to the Potawatomi Casino where he left his car parked.

Pumpkin's phone rang so much the battery was starting to die. Billy Gunz plugged it into his charger as soon as he got in his car. The phone was locked so he couldn't get in it or answer it. He made his next stop to the cellular store on 34th and Wells Street.

An Arab in his early forties stood behind a display cabinet and bulletproof glass. The display cabinet was stacked with all different types of cellphones. Knockoff clothes and shoes were displayed for sale on the walls around the shop. "Steve, what it do, baby!"

"Billy Gunz! What's up my buddy!!" Steve opened the door and came from behind the counter to shake his hand. "What are you doing here?"

"Just came to see a friend and ask for a small favor."

"Name it." He handed Steve the cellphone.

"Can you unlock this iPhone?"

"Can I unlock an iPhone? Of course, I can unlock it. I can unlock this in my sleep." Steve plugged the phone into his computer and two minutes later it was done. He wrote down the new passcode then handed it and the phone back to him. "You good now. The password is 3421."

"You the man Steve."

"I know. Come back and see me sometime."

"Will do." Billy Gunz gave him a two-finger salute and dipped out.

He sat in his car going through her phone. She had twenty-seven missed calls and nineteen text messages. The caller ID showed that most of the missed calls were from her moms and pops. While the majority of the text messages were from Cîroc, the texts from her parents were them worrying about where she was and why she wasn't answering her phone. Ciroc's text was asking if she took care of the business that Cutthroat told her to take care of. Then his text turned to why wasn't she answering the phone. Billy Gunz was tempted to hit Cîroc up and let him know he got his girl. But he felt it would be better to let him stew in his worry. It would knock him off his game making him more vulnerable to Billy Gunz's demands.

He powered her phone off knowing having it go straight to voicemail would intensify Ciroc's worry. Billy Gunz knew a worried mind equals cloudy thoughts and cloudy thoughts lead to mistakes. He needed Cîroc to make all the mistakes possible to make things that much easier for him to get rid of him.

He cranked the car up and hit the highway headed to Milwaukee's Shorewood neighborhood. He had to holla at Joey Long and it couldn't wait until tomorrow's meeting.

He calls K-Dolla's phone to get him to meet him there, but he got no answer. He tried a few more times and still no answer. Soon as he set the phone down on his lap, it rang. He picked it up and answered right away. "K-Dolla, where the hell you at? I've called your phone four times already."

"This ain't K-Dolla, this is Cowboy, Billy G." Billy Gunz moved the phone from his ear and looked at the caller ID. He saw that it was indeed Cowboy's number that called.

"My bad Cowboy, what's the word?"

"This crazy crack bitch woke up."

"So."

"So? That silly broad down there screaming her head off and trying to break the door down."

"Cowboy, I'm trying to get this stuff in order right now. I'm depending on you to keep things in check on that end. Come on now my nigga, don't act like you don't know how to calm down an irate crackhead. Handle that shit dog." Billy Gunz ended the call without giving Cowboy an opportunity to respond.

Making his exit off the highway he drove the streets until he reached the neighborhood straddled with mansions. Halfway down the block, he pulled into the long driveway that led to Joey Long's house. He got out of the car and rang the doorbell. A minute later the door opens a crack and Joey Long peeps his head out. "What's up dog?"

"We need to talk." Billy Gunz pushed the door open wider and pushed past Joey Long.

"It can't wait until tomorrow's meeting? I'm kind of in the middle of something." Billy Gunz walked to the center of the foyer and turned around to shoot him a reply but stopped when he saw the two half-naked women standing at the foot of the staircase. One was a petite little Asian woman, and the other was a blue-eyed brunette with big breast.

"Joey! Are we gonna go to bed or what?" The pouty brunette poked her butt out and the Asian girl smacked it to give him a tease.

"You ladies go upstairs; I'll be up there in a minute."

"Hurry up or we'll be a force to start without you." Joey Long watched the women playfully tickled each other as they scurried up the steps.

"Oh, Billy Boy, this better be good. I popped a pill and I ain't had a hard-on this strong since I was in my twenties. So, you better make it quick." Joey Long walked over to the bar and poured the two of them drinks. Then passed Billy Gunz one of the glasses. "So, what's so important it couldn't wait until tomorrow?"

"Corpus Christi." Joey Long's hand froze before the glass reached his lips.

"What about it?" Billy Gunz took a seat on the couch. Joey Long took a seat across from him in his favorite leather chair.

"Cîroc knows all about it."

"Impossible! How?" Billy Gunz sucked his teeth as he removed his Cartier frames.

"I believe he and his crew are secretly working for Cutthroat." A chuckle slowly came from Joey Long until it became a full-on laugh.

"Boy, you had me going for a minute. You come rushing over here talking about them lil niggas know about Corpus Christi had me spooked. Yo ass got a hell of a sense of humor."

"Joey, do it look like I'm trying to be funny? I'm dead ass serious. Cîroc knows about Corpus Christi and they're working for Cut." Joey Long saw the dangerously serious look on his face and knew he wasn't bullshitting.

"Billy that can't be. Cutthroat may have an ax to grind with you for that shit that happened in Texas, but he wouldn't ever stoop to that level of disloyalty. I mean for Christ's sake, y'all are brothers."

"So were Kane and Able. Dig this, wouldn't you agree that Cîroc and his team are some ruthless mothafuckas?" Joey Long shrugged his shoulders.

"Yeah, they remind me of how we used to get down when we were their age."

"And who taught us to be so ruthless back then?"

"Cutthroat."

"My point exactly!"

"Okay I can see the logic in that, but you still haven't convinced me that Joey is with them."

"I saw it with my own eyes."

"What exactly did you see?" Billy Gunz spilled out all the details for him and told him about him snatching up Pumpkin and locking her up in Cowboy's basement. "Yo I can't believe it. What is he trying to raise war against us for?"

"I think he wants to take over the streets and get revenge in the midst." Joey Long's nerve was starting to get the best of him. He stood up and began to pace the floor.

"And what do we supposed to do? Kill your brother? I can't do it. Cut is like a brother to me. I'm sure we can handle this shit in a more diplomatic way. How about offering him a spot at the table?

We both know he deserves that and more for what he has done for us."

"I agree he does." Billy Gunz thinks to himself a moment. The brunette woman appeared again at the top of the stairs.

"Joey! Come on, you're missing all the fun!"

"I'll be up there in a second. Get yo little ass back in that bed and wait for me." She sashayed her little pink booty back down the hall. Billy Gunz stood up and walked towards the front door.

"I'll talk to him about it and see what his response will be. But if he doesn't roll with that, then shit going to have to get real biblical. See you tomorrow."

Chapter 9

"Hello? Hello? Billy G? That black bastard hung up on me." Cowboy looks at the phone screen then puts it back into his pocket and cranks the radio up to drown up the yelling coming from the basement. The country sounds of Luke Bryan's song, That's My Kind Of Night, could be heard throughout the house. Cowboy tapped his foot to the music as he thought of what to do to keep Pumpkin from giving him trouble.

He exchanged his cowboy boots for tennis shoes and removed his belt and hat. He covered his face with a tiki mask he had from a party he threw last summer. Pumpkin used to buy dope from Cowboy and knew who he was from the neighborhood. Not knowing if Billy Gunz was going to kill her or let her go, he couldn't afford to have her recognize him. He didn't want to take any chances on retaliation that would come his way if Cîroc found out he had a hand in kidnapping Pumpkin.

He grabbed a couple of rocks of dope out of the smoke detector in the hallway. Then picked up the long barrel torch lighter he used to light candles with and started for the basement. Descending the basement steps, he could hear her yells for help over the music. Her foot banged over and over again on the steel door. Cowboy fished the keys out of his pocket and unlocked the deadbolt locks on the door.

The door exploded open hitting him in the head as Pumpkin attempted to push herself free. Cowboy quickly grabbed her by the waist and wrestled her back in the room and threw her on the cot. "Get your fucking hands off me!! Let me go!! Help!! Help!! Somebody help me!!" Pumpkin swung her fist wildly at him nearly knocking the mask off his face. He grabbed her arms and pinned her to the bed.

"Shut up!! I'm not gonna hurt you. But you keep acting like this I will tie your ass up and duct tape your mouth close. Do you understand me?" Cowboy told her trying his best to disguise his voice so she wouldn't recognize him.

"You know who you fucking with? You must not because if you did, you'll know how much of a dead man you'll be for this. My people ain't the kind of people you wanna cross. They'll kill everything you ever love and make you watch them suffer. It's in your best interest to let me go." She squirmed her arms and wrist trying to get free, but his grasp was too strong for her. His callous hands gripped her like vice grips made of flesh. "Look, you let me go right now there's no harm no foul and I won't tell anyone about this. If not, my peoples will hunt you down and kill you!" Cowboy leaned in closer to her until the lips of his mask were brushing against her cheek.

"I'll take my chances. Besides they can't come for you if they don't know where you are." He was right, no one knew where she was. Hell, she didn't even know where she was. That very thought alone scared her that much more. Afraid of him carrying out his threat to tie her up and duct tape her mouth shut, she stopped fighting him.

"Okay, okay, you win. Now let go of me." Cowboy released his grip and stepped back. Pumpkin scooted away to the other end of the bed resting her back against the wall. Her wrist ached where he had gripped her. She massaged the pain away from the best she could. "Who are you and what do you want with me?" She stared up at the mask on his face. Her piercing look made Cowboy nervous. To him, it felt as if she could see right through the mask and right in his face. He turned away.

"Who I am isn't important. What I want isn't what's keeping you here. But what my boss wants is."

"Who's your boss? What a minute, let me guess. Billy Gunz?" She didn't have to see his facial expression underneath the mask to get the answer to her question. A sudden turn of his head back in her direction told her she was right. "I figured. You tell that piece of shit Billy Gunz, he really fucked up now! My peoples are going to make him wish he was dead!" She laughed aloud, almost sinister-like. But her laugh was cut short by the pain in her head from where Billy Gunz hit her with the pistol. She winced and rubbed the knot on the back of her head. "I need some Tylenol or something, my head is pounding."

"I don't have any Tylenol or no shit like that. But I got something that might make you forget about the pain." Cowboy dug in his pocket and pulled out the two rocks he took out his stash and sat them on the bed. Her face frowned up as she looked down at the two packets of dope that were laid out in front of her.

"What the hell? Do I look like some dope head to you?" Cowboy knew she was fronting but played along with her.

"My apologies, I just thought you were a woman who didn't mind having a good time here and there. Besides this is all the medicine this pharmacy has. I'll take it away though if it's not your thing." He reached down to pick the two baggies up, but Pumpkin quickly snatched them away.

"I'll keep them for now. Just in case my headache doesn't go away anytime soon and becomes too much to bear. Anything is better than nothing."

"As you wish." Cowboy opened the door to leave but before closing the door he pulled the torch lighter out of his back pocket and tossed it on the bed. "You keep quiet and be a good girl and I'll keep you medicated. That is, if the pain becomes too much for you to bear. I know it would be a terrible thing if those headaches came back after the medicine wore off." He closed the door behind him and locked it before heading back upstairs.

Pumpkin fondled the two bags of dope in her hand. After five minutes she found herself busting open one of the bags spreading its crumbled contents on a Hustler magazine that lied on the bed. She reached in her bra and pulled out her crack pipe and loaded it up with the dope. She picked up the torch and took a long hard blast.

Cowboy closed the basement door and swiftly removed the mask from his face. It was hot underneath it and he had begun to sweat. Taking the sleeve of his shirt he wiped away the beads of sweat from his forehead. He turned the music down before going into the kitchen and pouring himself a glass of cold, cherry Kool-Aid that he made earlier that morning. In one giant gulp, he managed to drain half the glass. He took a hard look at the glass. "Ahhh! That's some damn good Kool-Aid right there."

No yelling and banging coming from the basement let him know feeding Pumpkin's habit was the best move to keep her under control. It wasn't his first rodeo with a dope fiend on a trip. And it wasn't his first time holding someone hostage for Billy Gunz.

Several years back, way before Trust and Ticky were on the scene, Cowboy was trying to earn his stripes to be on Billy Gunz's team. Only seven years younger than Billy Gunz he still looked up to him. He admired the respect Billy Gunz got from the streets. Being that Cowboy was always picked on, there wasn't anything more he wanted than to be amongst the respected.

Cats in the hood used to target him for bullying. They thought he was soft because of the way he dressed. Growing up in Albuquerque, New Mexico, the way he dressed was the norm. Girls out there loved the cowboy look and lifestyle. Being the only child and having a mother that worked at a department store that sold the best cowboy getup, he had all the latest boots and attire, making him the most popular kid around.

Sadly, when he was sixteen, he and his mother had to move to Milwaukee, Wisconsin to stay with his grandfather, due to his father dying from a fall he took from a ten-story building he was doing construction work on. His mother took a job as a supervisor at General Mills, a factory on the south side of town that made different types of breakfast cereals and other foods.

It didn't take long for Cowboy to realize just how far out of place he was living in Milwaukee. He quickly became the center of the wrong type of attention. The kids in the neighborhood used to tease him, chase him home from school, and beat him up. One bully, in particular, was a boy named Alonzo. Alonzo was two years older than Cowboy. He and his homeboys were also the popular assholes of the neighborhood.

Coming home from school one day Cowboy found himself unavoidably crossing paths with Alonzo and his boys. This time he'd had enough of running from them. This time he was going to stand his ground and fight like a man. Win or lose didn't matter to him at that point, he was just tired of running.

He balled up his fist as tight as he could and as soon as Alonzo ran up, he swung as hard as he could a clumsy punch. Alonzo ducked causing Cowboy to miss and fall to the ground. Then he and his boys took advantage of his fall and started stomping him. Cowboy reached down in his boot while they imprinted the bottom of their Nike's all over him. He pulled out a switchblade, pressed the button and began blindly wielding the knife at their legs. When they recognized he had a knife they backed off and started to run. Cowboy was too heated to let them get away. He ran after them with a knife in hand and blood dripping from his busted lip. Alonzo and his boys split up running in different directions, but Cowboy stayed focused on chasing down Alonzo. Alonzo had cut through a gangway, but his sagging jeans caused him to tumble over. He got back to his feet but before he could take another step Cowboy had tackled him back down to the ground. He pounded him repeatedly in the face with his fist busting Alonzo's nose. Still seeing red, Cowboy raised the knife but a hand had grabbed his arm and prevented him from plunging the blade into Alonzo's face.

"Easy there killa. Let me get this blade up out of you before you do something crazy." Billy Gunz pried the blade from Cowboy's tightly fisted hand.

"Kill this crazy mothafucka Billy Gunz!" Billy Gunz looked down at the battered face of Alonzo.

"Shut the fuck up. If you stop trying to bully everybody you wouldn't have to worry about me saving you from kissing the reaper. Let this be a lesson learned for you because next time I want to be here to save yo' stupid ass. Now get up and get the fuck up out of here." Alonzo pushed Cowboy off of him then got to his and ran off.

Billy Gunz flipped the blade close on the knife and handed it back to Cowboy. "I believe this belongs to you."

"Thanks." Cowboy took the knife and slipped it back into his boot.

"I've been having my eye on you lil dog. I've been waiting for you to show you had some heart. My homeboys didn't think you had it in you. But I knew you did. And because of their doubt, they just lost a lot of money to me. But that wasn't the only reason I've been waiting on you to show me the killa in you."

"Besides the wager with your buddies, why else?"

"So, I can offer you a job on my team. You down?" Billy Gunz held his hand out and Cowboy gladly shook his hand and accepted the opportunity.

Though when he accepted the job, he thought Billy Gunz was going to have him selling dope or transporting packs. But Billy Gunz had something completely different in mind for Cowboy. He made Cowboy one of his hitmen. Having him kidnap, torture, and kill anybody he felt he needed to make an example of.

After putting in so much work, to show his appreciation Billy Gunz gave him control over the spots on the east side. When that happened Cowboy became a true boss. He was respected in the hood and had enough clout that people knew not to fuck with him.

His reign on the east side came to an end shortly before Trust and Ticky took over. Trust was one of his workers and got busted by the police while making a drop off. Scared of having to do the five years' time the police was threatening him with, he told them all about Cowboy's operation in exchange for immunity. The cops raided Cowboy's spots and caught him with twelve ounces of powder cocaine. He was sentenced to eight years in the feds.

When he got out things weren't the same as they used to be. It was a whole new generation in play and that generation had no respect for the old ways. The new generation of hustlas weren't thinkers. They just didn't give a fuck and did things without planning it out. They had no problem recklessly opening fire in a crowd of children to try and get their target. More innocent people than targets become victims of their antics which is what made them in many people's eyes a dangerous threat. Cowboy was completely against spilling innocent blood that's why he always played the humble card with Cîroc instead of trying to go to war with him. He was hoping that with all the noise Cîroc and his crew were making in the streets that the feds would soon get them out the way and he could go back to hustling in peace. But with Billy Gunz having kidnapped Ciroc's girl things could get twisted into the very nightmare Cowboy had been trying to avoid. And all he could do in the meantime is keep his eyes open and his gun loaded.

King Dream

Chapter 10

Cutthroat's chromed-out chopper motorcycle growled as it pulled up in front of Ciroc's house. A man standing on the porch opened the front door and whistled loudly into the house. A short moment later Cîroc came outside shirtless with some Jersey shorts and Jordans on. Sweat poured down his torso. He walked over to Cutthroat who was still sitting on the motorcycle. Cîroc handed him a fat stack of money he pulled out his pocket. It was his cut of the profits Cîroc and his crew makes. They all worked for Cutthroat. Cutthroat was the leader of the No Love No Mercy crew. Cîroc was his number one soldier. He put him in charge of the clique while he played in the shadows. Though all major moves such as who they could kill or who they could rob had to get Cutthroat's approval first.

Cutthroat met Cîroc through Pumpkin a couple of years before he got released from the feds. Cîroc used to come along with Pumpkin and a couple of others when they would go visit him in the joint. At first, Cutthroat was skeptical about him and grilled him every chance he got. Once he got comfortable with his presence and getting to know him, they grew close. Eventually, he had Cîroc coming to visit him by himself. On those visits, he would break down his plans of taking over the streets and tell Cîroc what he wanted him and his crew to do. They followed his orders like true soldiers putting a new fear in the hearts of the people in the city. Cutthroat couldn't have been prouder of Cîroc as his soldier. With dedication like that on his side, he felt there could be nothing that could stop him from prying the streets from the hands of Billy Gunz and The Order. No Love No Mercy was going to send The Order into retirement one way or another.

"Wassup Cut?" Cutthroat pulled down his COVID-19 mask so he could be heard clearly.

"Where's Pumpkin and why isn't she answering the phone?"

"I was hoping you would have that answer. I've been blowing her line up all day."

"You mean to tell me you don't know where she's at?"

"Last I checked she was with you. I dropped her off myself."

"She came to the house and left back out saying she was going to run to the store. That was hours ago. And she's not answering the phone."

"I'm just as worried as you Cut." Cutthroat looked him up and down.

"Yeah, you look really worried. You out here playing basketball while Pumpkin could be missing."

"That's how I clear my head so I could think clearly enough to focus on where she could be." Cutthroat pounded his fist on the motorcycle's gas tank.

"God damn it! I was hoping she was with you. I think she may have run."

"What do you mean she may have run?" Cutthroat began to explain what happened before Pumpkin left the house.

"I don't know if you are aware or not, but for some time now Pumpkin's been fighting a crack addiction."

"I knew it!" Cutthroat had finally confirmed his suspicion about Pumpkin's secret habit.

"Before she left the house, we were discussing her going to rehab."

"Let me guess, she was against it?"

"Nah, she was all for it. She said she was ready to get the help she needed to kick the habit. She seemed like she meant it. I guess that dope got more control over her than she thought. We need to find her Cîroc, ASAP."

"I'm on it." Cutthroat's phone rang. He got off the bike and dug it out of his pocket. Looking at the screen, he saw it was Billy Gunz calling. He answers.

"What do you want Billy?"

"Didn't pops teach you better phone manners than that, bruh?"

"Yeah, right before he taught me how to hang up on annoying callers. You want me to show you how it's done?"

"Relax, I'm calling with good news."

"What news might that be?" Cutthroat leaned against his motorcycle and lit up a cigarette.

"I talked with the rest of The Order and we decided to offer you a seat on the board with us."

"I seat on the board, isn't that generous of you all." He shook his head and blew out a cloud of cigarette smoke.

"You don't sound too pleased with the offer."

"Why should I be when it's being offered by the biggest snake I have ever known? I've been out of the joint for three years. Why offer me such an important position now?"

"The board and I recognize we were in the wrong for waiting so long to offer you a seat at the table and we want to correct that."

"Spoken like a true man of business. It is sad that you could speak to me like that. That further lets me know you still haven't learned how to put family over money. So, you take your little offer and shove it deep up yo ass until you could taste the bullshit you so full of." The phone went silent for several seconds. Then Cutthroat heard the sound of Billy Gunz sucking on his gold teeth. It was a habit he had that showed whenever he was nervous, upset, or deep in thought. Cutthroat knew at that moment Billy Gunz was feeling all of the above.

"Look here, you don't want to take my offer, then fine. Be that way you stubborn son of a bitch. I'm going to tell you one thing though, you and this little clique you have with Cîroc better stand the fuck down. Yeah, I know all about that. You weren't worried about them taking over the streets because they work for you."

Billy Gunz could hear Cutthroat clapping his hands on the other end of the phone.

"It's about time you figured that out. I was starting to think for a minute you were a little slow in the head."

"Brother or no brother, you and your people keep trying to come for me and I'm going to show you mothafuckas just how ruthless I can be."

"Oh, little brother I can't wait to see." Billy Gunz ended the call without another word spoken. Cutthroat looked over at Cîroc with a small smirk on his face. "It seems like my little brother found out the truth about us."

"So, what do we do now?"

"Well now that our enemy knows who exactly he's at war with we give him no time to plan or think ahead. We hit them with full force from every angle leaving them with no option but to surrender or die." Ciroc's phone beeps with a picture message from Pumpkin's phone. "About time she reached back."

"That's Pumpkin?"

"Yeah." He opened the message and a picture of Pumpkin laid out on a filthy cot in what looked like someone's basement. The message that came with the picture read:

I guess I'm going to have to show you and your boss just how ruthless his little brother can get...

Cutthroat saw Ciroc's eyes grow wide with shock.

"What is it?" Cîroc couldn't say anything he just passed the phone to him. Cutthroat's heart sank when he saw the picture and read the message. He immediately began dialing Pumpkin's phone. Billy Gunz picked up the line on the third ring.

"I'm sorry, Cîroc. If you were looking for Pumpkin, she can't get to the phone right now."

"You touch that girl, Billy, and I'll kill you!"

"Oh, this Cut. You must be with Cîroc because the caller ID says this is his number you're calling from. I don't care to speak with you over the phone, Cut. Your phone manners are terrible. You have a habit of pissing me off over the phone. With that bitch in my possession the last thing you need is for me to get pissed."

"Then let's talk in person."

"Fair enough. Meet me at Fade Masters Barbershop."

"I'll be there in twenty minutes."

"See you when you get here, big bro." He handed Cîroc back his phone once the call ended.

"With all due respect, Cut, I swear no matter what you say, if your brother harms a single hair on her head, I will kill him!"

"You would have to beat me to it. Follow me to Fade Masters." Cîroc nodded his then looked towards the house where Wild-Child was posted.

"Wild-Child, hold shit down until I get back. I got some business to take care of. Stay on point." Overhearing the whole conversation between Cîroc and Cutthroat, Wild-Child was aware of why he told him to stay on point.

"I got this bruh, and if you need me to come aid and assist, hit my line and I'll be there blasting with no questions asked." Cutthroat pulled his mask back over the bottom half of his face and cranked up his motorcycle. He revved the engine and the pipes growled loudly. He pulled off into traffic. Cîroc followed close behind in his drop-top BMW.

When they got to the barbershop, Billy Gunz Rolls-Royce was parked out front. Cutthroat didn't know why but even just the sight of his car pissed him off even more. They parked in the parking lot beside the barbershop and got out. "Cîroc, the nigga standing out front on the phone."

"That nigga Pay Pay?"

"Yeah, make sure he stays outside. He moves a muscle, blow his brains out."

"My pleasure." When they got close to the door Pay Pay put his phone away and attempted to follow in behind them. Cîroc stopped letting the door close shut behind Cutthroat. Then turned around with his 45 in hand pointed at Pay Pay. "How about you and I chill out here a minute while the old heads sort out their family issues." He had caught Pay Pay off guard leaving him no choice but to stay where he was.

Inside, Billy Gunz chopped it up with a couple of his friends as his barber lined him up. The whole shop was in the midst of laughing at a joke he told them about a priest caught with his dick stuck in a statue of a virgin Mary, when the door swung open. A smile creased Billy Gunz's face when he saw Cutthroat's mugged-up face walk through the door. "There goes my big brother, Cut." Cut didn't say a word. He stormed towards Billy Gunz with a 44-snub nose in hand. He squeezed off two shots shooting both men in the thigh that sat in barber chairs on each side of Billy Gunz. The men fell over moaning and covering their wounds with their hands. Everyone inside ducked and took cover. He then pointed the gun at Billy Gunz's head. "Pointing a loaded gun at my head. Damn, Cut, why you got to be so disrespectful? Can't we just talk like a normal family?"

"Where the fuck is she, Billy?" Billy Gunz spun his chair around to take a look at his lining in the mirror.

"First you tell me something. I can see why this dope-smoking bitch would mean something to Cîroc. But why you so concerned about her? Is it because she's a member of your crew and you love her like family? Or y'all got some type of freaky shit going on?"

"She's my daughter!" Billy Gunz stopped brushing the hairs of his goatee and froze for a moment. He turned his chair back around to look him in the face.

"Nice try, but I know you better than anyone. And I know you don't have any kids."

"Then you don't know me as well as you thought you did. Her mother is Debbie."

"The girl you met at the Jam 4 Peace concert."

"Yeah, I found out she was pregnant a couple of days before all that shit went down in Texas."

"Wow, that's quite the shocker. I see now I got a bargaining chip you can't refuse. Take the offer I told you about over the phone and I'll release her."

"You bitch ass nigga. I'm telling you the girl that you got locked away in some basement is your niece and you still trying to make a deal for her life?"

"Like you said, I've never been too big on putting family over business."

"Billy, you hurt my baby and I will murder that pink face bitch of yours and those half-breed kids y'all have together." Billy Gunz scooted to the edge of his seat and looked his older brother dead in the eyes with an emotionless face.

"I don't doubt that one bit. But you got to ask yourself, do I really give a fuck? I'm wealthy and healthy with strong swimming sperm. I can always find a new bitch to replace her and make more kids without shedding a single tear for the ones I lost. Can you do the same?"

"There's no way you could be that heartless, Billy." Billy Gunz stood up. Cutthroat pulled back the hammer on his revolver. Billy Gunz walked right up to the gun letting the barrel press against his forehead.

"Try me and see." Cutthroat could see in his eyes he was serious. That made him want so badly to pull the trigger and blow Billy Gunz's brains out all over the mirror behind him. His hand shook a little with an itch to squeeze the trigger. Before that itch grew too much to resist, he disarmed the hammer and lowered the gun.

"I accept your offer. Now release my daughter."

"I will, but not until you and your crew hand over all the money y'all stole from the spots that belonged to The Order. I estimate that to be around two hundred thousand, give or take." Billy Gunz was getting over on him and he knew it. It couldn't have been any more than a hundred thousand that they had broken his spots off for, everything else came from other spots. It didn't matter, he could have the money. All Cutthroat was concerned with right then was getting Pumpkin back.

"Give me a few days to scrape that change up."

"You got until Sunday. 2 days. Any more time than that and she becomes a burden that I would be forced to rid myself of in a way you wouldn't be too pleased with."

"You'll have your money. But you bet not let shit happen to her." Billy Gunz crossed his heart.

"You got my word." Cutthroat tucked his gun in the waist of his pants and walked out of the barbershop.

"Let's roll, Cîroc." He walked past and jumped on his motor-cycle.

"It's been nice holding you hostage, Pay Pay. Let me leave you with a small piece of advice. Try learning more about history. Especially your father's. You'll be amazed at what you find." Cîroc flashed a devious smile and walked off.

Chapter 11

Pay Pay sat in the living room of his mama's house going through the family photo album again. This time he was looking specifically for pictures of his father.

While Billy Gunz and Cutthroat were inside the barbershop, Pay Pay listened as Cîroc went on and on about how the future could never keep the past buried. Pay Pay thought the little nigga was high and wasn't making any sense. Though he couldn't shake from his head what Cîroc had last said to him, about knowing his father's history. He thought it might sound crazy, but could Cîroc possibly know something about his father's past. For that reason only, he sat with every family album on the table in front of him. He didn't know why exactly he felt finding pictures of his father would give him more insight into things he didn't know about him, but he was determined to go through every last picture of him with the hope that something might catch his attention.

His father loved taking photos. It was his way of immortalizing the good times. His ever-indulging good times had Pay Pay, twenty-five minutes later, still going through pictures. His eyes had begun to hurt from looking at so many pictures. Just as he was about to call it quits, he turned to the last page in one of the photo albums and something familiar caught his eye. The picture wasn't anything out of the ordinary, just a picture of his father and mother hugging each other at the airport. A sign in the background let him know it was the O'Hare Airport in Chicago. What caught his attention about it was a black alligator skin briefcase his father was carrying. The same briefcase he took with him when he left town and gave to Resa every time he came back. The sight of it brought back a memory for him.

A memory of him playing a game of Tag at the park across the street from his house. He was it and trying to tag another kid from the neighborhood when he noticed his father's big body, silver Cadillac with white half top, leaving from the house. He was having so much fun playing he didn't even see his father come to the house. He knew it couldn't have been long since his father was at the house. He had just got back from a business trip and Pay Pay was hoping he wasn't going back out of town before he got a chance to see him.

Pay Pay abandoned his game of tag and ran to the crib to find out what was going on. He opened the screen door and ran through the house searching for his mama. Upstairs he saw the attic steps had been lowered. The attic was finished and set up as a workshop for his mother to pursue her hobby of designing clothes. Pay Pay ascended the steps and saw Resa stuffing that same alligator skin briefcase into a hidden cubbyhole in the wall of the attic. "Mama?" Resa got startled as he was caught by surprise.

"Boy, you scared the bejeezus out of me." She put her hand over her heart and caught her breath.

"What are you doing?"

"Up here working, baby."

"What's that?" He came closer and pointed to the cubbyhole. Resa quickly covered the hole with the false wall.

"It's nothing. Just mama's secret hidden spot. A little place I keep things I don't want no one else to find."

"Not even daddy?"

"Not even your daddy. The only one who knows about this spot is me and now you. But you got to keep this a secret. Don't tell anyone about this and don't ever go in here. Can I count on you to do that?"

"Yes, ma'am." Resa ruffled his hair with her hand and smiled at him.

"Good, let's go downstairs and get dinner started before your father gets back." That was all he remembered of that day. But it

was all he needed to remember to know where he might find what he was looking for.

Lucky for him, his mother refused his many offers of moving to a fancier neighborhood. She still lived in the same house they did when he was a kid. Pay Pay headed straight for the attic. He pulled the cord that released the stairs that lead to his mother's old workshop. A cloud of dust fogged the air when he positioned the dusty staircase into place. At the top of the stairs, he was met with thick strains of spider webbing that accumulated over the years. Using his hand, he swapped the webbing out of his way and flipped on the light switch. The room lit up and everything came into view.

Mannequins dressed in some of his mother's fashion creations nearly scared him when the lights came on. Over the years, Resa had done a few remodeling upgrades to the house but the attic remained untouched. Everything was left the way it was the day his father died. Even her sewing machine still had the same sparkling emerald-green dress she was working on that day in it.

Pay Pay went to the back of the attic, to the wall behind the desk that her sewing machine sat on. It took some effort but with a little effort, he was able to remove the false wall. Behind the false wall was a large safe. Pay Pay tried turning the lever but the safe was locked. The combination dial was left on the number 5. The number left him stuck, he had no clue what it meant. He tried a few meaningless combinations he thought it could be but neither worked. He got up and paced the floor as he thought hard on what the combination could be.

A picture of Pay Pay and his parents sat in a frame on his mama's work desk. The silver frame had the words, *"FAMILY BE MY ALL."* Then it dawned on him what the combination code could be. He rushed back over to the safe and began turning the dial. He quickly spun the dial to 06-15-05, this time when he turned the lever the safe opened up. The combination stood for the letters

FOE. It was an abbreviation for his father's motto, Family Over Everything. A motto he lived by until the day he died.

Inside the safe was bricks of money wrapped in a cream wrap, a sawed-off Mossberg shotgun, miscellaneous jewels, and two gold 45's fitted with extended clips. The alligator skin briefcase wasn't there, but barely visible to the naked eye was a folder hidden underneath the bricks of money. Pay Pay pulled the folder out and opened it up.

The folder contained documents of various investments and bank accounts. Hidden between some bank statements were his father's death certificate and autopsy report. He pulled it out and looked over it. It was his first time ever seeing it. When he got to the autopsy report and he looked down at the cause of death, he found the first piece of evidence that shined a light of truth to his suspicion. At that point, Pay Pay knew for a fact his father's past was a lot deeper than he had ever imagined. Furthermore, Pay Pay was determined to reach the depths of it.

The front door opened as he sat on the couch nursing a bottle of Grey Goose vodka. In came Noodles, Dayla, and his mama with shopping bags in hand, laughing and talking loud. "Hey, bae." Noodles leaned over and gave him a kiss, then sat down Dayla and the bags she had in her hand.

"Hey, sweetie. I'm surprised to see you home so early. I thought you had some things to take care of today." Resa sat her bags.

"My investors had a busy schedule, so our meeting was brief, and I was able to wrap business up a little earlier than usual today."

"Then you decided to come home and stare at a bunch of old pictures?" She pointed to the photo albums sprawled out all over the living room.

"Nah, I came back to search for the truth."

"Truth about what?"

"The truth about my father and how he died."

"What you mean *how he died*? You know how he died in a car accident." Pay Pay jumped to his feet.

"That's bullshit mama and you know it!" Noodles looked at Pay Pay in shock at how mad he seemed to be at his mama. She knew whatever it was had to be serious and nothing Dayla should hear.

"I think I'll take Dayla across the street to the park so you two can talk. Come on baby, let's go play on the swings." Noodles picked Dayla up and left out. Resa walked up to Pay Pay and paused a moment to stare into his eyes. Then she brought her hand across his face slapping a spittle of liquor from his mouth.

"Now I don't know if it's this liquor " She snatches the bottle out his hand and holds it up. "that got you feeling a certain way right now." She then slammed the bottle down on the coffee table. "But boy if you ever talk to me like that again I will take you out of this world as quickly as I brought you in it. You understand me?" Pay Pay rubbed his cheek.

"I apologize. But I'm not gonna let you keep hiding the truth from me. I want to know what happened to my father."

"What makes you think something other than what I told you happened to him?" Pay Pay reached over and grabbed the autopsy report off the end table and gave it to her.

"Because the coroner says right there that the cause of death was ruled a homicide. He says my father had seven bullets in him." Resa closed her eyes for a brief moment and slowly let out a heavy sigh. "For whatever reason, you've been keeping everything from me. Now is the time you come clean with me. It's time for me to know the truth about my father." Resa went into the kitchen then returned with two empty glasses and a pack of Kool 100 cigarettes.

"Well, if we're going to discuss the past, then neither one of us should be sober." She sat down next to him on the couch and filled their glasses with the Grey Goose vodka. "Bobby wasn't a business analyst; he was the biggest Kingpin in the United States."

"Never. I ain't ever heard the streets mention pop's name as being a cat that ran the city, let alone the whole country."

"That's because not many people knew it. Bobby was smart and played in the shadows of the game. He didn't want the fame that came with it. He always said it was the fame that got a person knocked by the feds or killed. Only his crew and his suppliers knew he was the one running things." Resa paused a moment to light a cigarette.

"I thought you stopped smoking?"

"I did, I just keep a pack around for times like this."

"Tell me what happened the day he died?"

"That part I honestly don't know. The two of you were together and I was here working on designing a new dress for a fashion show."

"I was there? I don't remember that."

"You were young. He took you down to Texas to meet your Aunt Edna and your cousin, Martin." While he was down there, he had to meet up with one of his suppliers, so he left you with Edna. The next thing I know I was getting a call from Edna telling me that he and a few others were dead in what looked to be a drug deal gone wrong."

"What about his crew, they weren't there to help him? They never told you what went down?"

"Baby, I don't know nothing about his crew, and they didn't know me. Your daddy treated the streets and home like church and state and stayed cautious not to ever let the two meet. He never kept any drugs in the house or let anyone know where he lived. He kept another house and another bitch on the other side of town."

"Wait a minute. Pops had another woman, and you knew about it?"

"Knew about it? It was my idea. It was an illusion we needed to keep people from finding out where The Bread-Man kept his heart. Which was another reason he stayed gone so much. It was his way of keeping us safe." Pay Pay drained his drink and poured up another.

"The Bread-Man?"

"That was his street name." Pay Pay picked up the picture of his father and mother hugging at the airport.

"If he never brought drugs home, then what was in that alligator skin briefcase he used to give you whenever he came home?"

"You remember that?"

"It's what made me remember your secret cubbyhole."

"The briefcase contained money he used to have me stash in the cubbyhole safe until he could get a bulk of it transferred to one of our bank accounts in the Cayman Islands." She took a puff of her cigarette. "I ain't seen that old briefcase since he left. The police never recovered it either. So, whoever killed him had to have been the one who stole it." Pay Pay shook his head in disbelief at the revelation his mother just gave him. She was definitely blowing his mind.

"I can't believe you've been lying to me all these years. I thought we always kept it one-hundred with each other, mama?"

"I never told you because I knew your father wouldn't want you to know that side of his life. He was your hero. I wanted him to continue to be that positive role model you looked up to. But don't try and throw a guilt trip on me, acting like you haven't been lying to me as well."

"Lying to you about what?"

"About you being a damn investment banker!" Pay Pay turned his head away in shame. "I ain't blind or dumb. I know you're in the drug game. I just pray that, unlike your father, you make a safe exit out. Don't let me or Noodles have to explain to Dayla when she gets older of your past and why you're not with her like I'm having to do for your father right now." The front door open and Noodles stepped halfway in.

"Is it safe to come in?" Resa waved them in.

"Come on in here so I can feed my grandbaby. I know she had to have done worked up an appetite with all that playing." Noodles walked in holding Dayla's hand. Resa looked over at Pay Pay who was still deep in thought trying to digest all he heard. "Now you know the truth."

Chapter 12

Billy Gunz tapped his fingers on the table. For the eighth time in the last fifteen minutes, he checked the time on his Rolex. His patience was draining by the second and his paranoia was amping up. "This ain't like K-Dolla to not return our calls or be late for a meeting. Something's up, and I can bet my bottom dollar Cutthroat and his crew is behind it." Two chairs down sat Joey Long twirling a toothpick around in his mouth. He pulled the toothpick out his mouth before giving Billy Gunz his thoughts.

"Let's not jump to any conclusions Billy. K-Dolla may never have been late for a meeting, but we both know how caught up he gets at those church events. I swear, sometimes when that nigga get to preaching, he thinks he's the prophet of God himself."

"Amen to that," Missy added in from her seat next to Billy Gunz. Billy Gunz's office door opened up, and in walked K-Dolla.

"Pardon my tardiness."

"Where the hell have you been? I've been trying to reach you since yesterday?" K-Dolla takes a seat next to Joey Long.

"My bad Billy G, my phone must've fallen out my pocket in the limo on the way to the church event. And the event went on longer than I expected. By the time Victoria and I got back to the hotel, we were both too tired to do anything but sleep. But I'm here now." Joey Long slapped his hand on the table then opened his arms to express his point.

"What I tell you? The great prophet Dolla was caught up in character as usual." Billy Gunz turned his head from Joey Long to K-Dolla.

"That's all it was K-Dolla, you lost track of time entertaining?" K-Dolla chuckled.

"You know me, Billy G. When the spirit takes ahold, I put on one hell of a show and don't know when to stop."

"You right about one thing, I do know you." Billy Gunz stared K-Dolla down with narrow eyes, trying to read him. "Where's Victoria?"

"She wasn't feeling well so I told her to stay in bed and I'll come then fill her in on everything when I get back." Billy Gunz's eyes continued piercing through K-Dolla making him feel like a hooker in church.

"You sure everything's alright?" K-Dolla straightened the jacket of his suit and sat up straight.

"Yeah, everything's cool. Now fill me in on what I missed." Billy Gunz eased his gaze and leaned back in his chair. Seeing Billy Gunz relax K-Dolla was able to calm his nerves and breathe a little. Billy Gunz began getting him up to speed on what's been going on.

"That explains why you opted out of calling Pay Pay and Noodles to attend this meeting. You say we're supposed to make the exchange tomorrow? Where are you stashing the girl at until then?"

"Does it matter?"

"Not at all. I'm just a curious mind that wants to be in the know." Billy Gunz's eyes wandered from Joey Long to Missy, wondering whether or not they were picking up on the same vibes he was. Joey Long hadn't seemed to take notice of K-Dolla's strange demeanor. Missy was aware though. She nodded her head inconspicuously at Billy Gunz letting him know her antennas were up. Billy Gunz turned his gaze back to K-Dolla.

"You should watch yourself Dolla, you know what they say about curiosity." K-Dolla swallowed hard and fixed his tie, trying his best to disguise his fear. Fear made a man nervous, and nervousness would make him look to be guilty of something. Those were signs he didn't want Billy Gunz to see in him. If he smelled the fear on him, he was as good as dead. Billy Gunz's next move made K-Dolla realize he wasn't doing a good job of masking his fear. Billy Gunz casually pulled his 9mm from his holster and pointed it towards K-Dolla. K-Dolla throws his hands up.

"Come on Billy, what are you doing?" He shut his eyes as tight as he could in fear of what was coming next. The next sound he heard was a click. He opened his eyes and saw that it was only the sound of Billy Gunz pressing the magazine release button and the clip sliding out. Billy Gunz then slid back the slide of the gun ejecting the bullet from the chamber. He opened a case that sat next to him and pulled out a wire brush and solution and began cleaning the gun. Then a mischievous smile crept upon Billy Gunz's face.

"You a little jumpy ain't you Dolla?" You should really get some rest playa. You seem a little uneasy today." K-Dolla pulled out his handkerchief and wiped the sweat from his neck.

"Yeah, well I can't argue with that, right? I can use a few days of relaxation. Between preaching and hustling I've been running around like a chicken with its head chopped off." K-Dolla poured himself a glass of water from the glass picture on the table.

"A vacation could certainly do you some good. Don't worry about the girl, she's safe. I got her stored in the last place Cut or Cîroc would think to find her. She's under lock and key at that old club that used to be a factory, over there on Teutonia Avenue and Florist."

"The old 414 Club?"

"That's the one."

"I'm familiar with it. Dig this though. You ain't really going to kill the girl if he doesn't come through with all the money, are you? I mean she is your niece." Billy Gunz shot a quizzical look at him.

"Why wouldn't I? I don't know the little bitch. I got more love for her daddy than I do for her and I'll kill his ass quicker than you could blink an eye. You've been in this game with me long enough, Dolla, to know how I play it. It's MOE with me. Money Over Everybody." Billy Gunz pulled the wire brush out of the barrel then squeezed the trigger causing the slide to slide back into its normal position. He put some of the gun cleaner on a rag to polish the gun up with.

"Whoa, that's some cold-hearted shit."

"It's a cold world. Don't tell me you getting too weak to adapt?"

"Never that."

"Let's hope not." Billy Gunz noticed K-Dolla's leg moved anxiously every time he checked the time, which had been every five minutes since he got there.

"You got somewhere you need to be Dolla?"

"I got to get back to check on the wifey, make sure she's doing alright."

"I can understand that. So, if there's nothing more to be said this meeting is adjourned." K-Dolla swiftly down his glass of water.

"Alright, I'll see you fellas tomorrow. " Billy Gunz watched K-Dolla like a hawk watching its prey, as he got up and left the room. Missy left right behind him. Joey long took the toothpick out his mouth.

"I thought you said you got that girl stored at Cowboy's pad?"

"I do."

"Then you want to fill me in on whatever it is I'm missing?"

"If I got to fill you in, then you must be losing your touch. You ain't notice how funny K-Dolla was acting? How he kept checking the time on his watch? And let's say he did lose his phone in the limo, as he says he did, why not use Victoria's phone to check in with us?"

"That is a little suspicious. And now that you mention it, he did seem really nervous. And sweating more than usual too." Joey Long pointed his toothpick at Billy Gunz as he spoke.

"I'm telling you something is up with him. And I think I might have an idea of just what it is too." Billy Gunz tossed the rag to the side then slipped the clip back into the butt of the gun and loaded a bullet into the chamber. He then stood up and returned the gun back to its holster while walking over to the window. He watched as K-Dolla jumped into a rental car and took off like a bat out of hell. He turned his head and saw Joey Long was standing next to him. "Not really Dolla's style, even for a rental car, don't you think?"

"Absolutely not. You think we should trail him and find out where he's headed?"

"Nah, the way he dipped up out of here, he'll be long gone into another county before you could make it out of the driveway. Besides, if I'm right we're about to find out real soon just what our boy reverend Dolla's been up to."

"Okay. But you know I know you were bluffing, right? I know you since we were shorties and I know damn well you're not going to kill your own niece."

"Of course not. But I needed him to believe I would."

"I get where going with this." Billy Gunz put his hand on Joey Long's shoulder.

"Then say we go put the cheese in the trap so we can catch ourselves a rat." Joey Long discarded his toothpick in the small waste bin next to the bookshelf.

"K-Dolla is like our brother, so for this once I pray our trap comes up empty."

"And if it doesn't?"

"Then I'm going to cut that nigga's nuts off myself for having the balls to cross us."

"I know a store with knives surgically sharp enough to get the job done. We'll stop there along the way." Billy Gunz winked his eye at him, and they headed out to put their plans in motion.

King Dream

Chapter 13

With sweat racing down his face, K-Dolla checked the time on his watch as he sped out of Billy Gunz's driveway. He had less than thirty minutes to get back to the location they were keeping Victoria. Her life was at stake if he didn't make it back before the time was up. Not ever wanting to live life without the woman he loved, K-Dolla stormed through the streets and onto the highway.

Once he hit the highway, he put the pedal to the metal on the 2000 Dodge Intrepid. He dipped around a few cars and got stuck between a semi-truck on each side of him. A small smart car with a Geek Squad logo on it was in front of him causing him to slow down. The Geek Squad car was going the exact speed limit of 55 miles per hour. K-Dolla couldn't go around the car because the semi-trucks were unintentionally blocking him in. He pressed down on the gas until he was riding the bumper of the tiny car in front of him. He hit his horn repeatedly and stuck his head out the window to yell at the driver. "Man, put a whip to that damn horse or get the hell out my way!!" Instead of speeding up the guy in the Geek Squad car decided to be an asshole and kept tapping on his breaks every time K-Dolla got close to his bumper. K-Dolla was getting pissed off and had no time to play with the man. He had less than seventeen minutes to be back at the spot. He sped up just as the semi to the right of him had taken the next exit. He jumped to the right lane and as he did so the asshole jumped back in front of him before he could accelerate. K-Dolla hit the gas anyway smashing the little car off the side of the highway.

With his front bumper leaning slightly to the right and right headlight hanging, he continued pushing the car to the max. He flew through the underpass so fast he didn't see the highway patrol car ducked off on the side of it.

As soon as K-Dolla blew past him his speedometer gun went off, clocking him at 103 miles per hour. The tires of the patrol car spent kicking up dust and gravel making its way from the side of the road and onto the highway with its sirens blaring. K-Dolla witnessed the flashing blue and red lights in the rearview mirror. He looked down at the time on the car's radio clock. "Damn! I don't need this shit right now!" He had less than fourteen minutes left and was still eighteen minutes away from his location. Before he could even get there, he had to shake the highway patrol off his ass, because if he showed up with cops on his tail Victoria would still be good as dead.

K-Dolla had a good half a mile distance on the highway patrol but that distance was closing fast. K-Dolla came up fast on the bumper of a Coca-Cola truck. He blindly made a swift switch to the left lane accelerating hard to get around the Coca-Cola truck and nearly ran into the back of a small camper. He quickly slowed down and turned back into the middle lane behind the Coca-Cola truck. He steered a little to the right to get a glimpse of what the right lane looked like. He saw that it was good and changed lanes. The patrol car caught up and was able to nick the back of his bumper as he changed lanes nearly making the Dodge Intrepid spin out of control. K-Dolla gripped the steering wheel tight and gained control of the car. The highway patrol officer was now side by side with him. The officer got on his loudspeaker. "Pull Over!" K-Dolla looked over at the drill sergeant-looking patrolman with the buzz cut and shook his head no, then gave him the middle finger. The patrolman's face balled up and turned red at his vulgar hand gesture. Then he jerked the wheel to the right trying to push him off the road but K-Dolla saw it coming ahead of time and hit the gas. The Intrepid lurched forward and the patrol car missed it by inches and side-swiped a guardrail.

A light ticking sound was coming from under the hood of the Intrepid but K-Dolla ignored it and kept pushing forward as fast as the car would go. The patrol car was still on his ass and now four more squad cars had joined the chase but not yet caught up. The ticking sound got louder, it sounded like someone was shaking a metal bolt inside a tin can. K-Dolla didn't know what it was and didn't care, all that mattered was him getting back to Victoria in time.

The patrolman with the buzz cut rammed him from behind making K-Dolla's body lurch forward. "This mothafucka just won't give up!" K-Dolla said to himself. He checked traffic to the left of him in the side-view mirror. He was clear for the lane switch. Instead of going one lane over, he switched all the way over to the third lane.

Ding! Ding! Ding! The engine light lit up on the dash and the coolant temperature gauge began floating over to the H and into the red. The car was starting to overheat. There was no way K-Dolla could ignore the ticking sound. It now made the car sound like a mad diesel truck going full throttle uphill. Buzzcut got behind him, this time he had enough of playing games with K-Dolla. Buzzcut held his police-issued Glock out the window and fired off five shots at the Intrepid. Three bullets pierced the back windshield and came out the front one. The shattering of glass made K-Dolla duck behind the wheel then switch to the middle lane. The engine rattled harder and two of the motor mounts broke and the engine started shaking terribly. Smoke raised from under the hood. "Come on baby, you can make it." K-Dolla coached the car as the engine light dinged and the engine rattled louder.

It was no way the car was going to make it much farther and K-Dolla was still three exits away from his exit. He had to shake the highway patrol cars.

Another cruiser caught up to the chase. The new cruiser took up the right lane. Both he and Buzzcut's cruisers were lined up with the Intrepid. K-Dolla knew exactly what they were trying to do. "No, no, no. Trick no good bitch." Both cruisers simultaneously attempted to side smash the Intrepid to sandwich it in, but K-Dolla smashed on the brakes making the two cars side smash each other. The front passenger's wheel of Buzzcut's cruiser got caught in the other cruiser's bumper guard. Buzzcut tried jerking the wheel to the left to free his car, but his plan backfired on him. Both cruisers veered off the road hitting a median and flipping over several times before Buzzcut's vehicle came to rest upside down on the opposite side of the highway and the other cruiser in a ditch.

K-Dolla laughed at the wreckage. Putting the pedal to the floor he got the car up to 96 MPH before it began stuttering to go faster. He was now two exits away with the three remaining cruisers closing in. He pumped his foot on the gas pedal hoping that would get it going faster. Instead Puff!! Thick clouds of smoke came from under the hood obscuring his view through the windshield for several moments. When the smoke thinned out, he could see half a mile up the road highway patrol was preparing to lay a spike strip.

K-Dolla didn't notice the car's engine was no longer knocking. He pressed down on the gas and nothing. The car didn't move, it just continued coasting down the highway. He looked down at the dash and saw every light on and the engine wasn't running. He threw the car in neutral and attempted to start it. When he turned the key all it made was a clicking noise. K-Dolla's granddaddy was a master mechanic who he spent a lot of summers working with as a kid. It was no doubt to him what was wrong with the car. The aluminum motors Dodge put in that model Intrepid were garbage and couldn't take much abuse. And as hard as K-Dolla was riding it was no surprise the engine both threw a rod and blew a head gasket.

K-Dolla was losing momentum fast, his speed had dropped to 73 MPH and on a steady decline. He was coming up on the next exit, but he still had another exit to go to be closer to his destination. But he had no choice, his best chance of getting away was to take the upcoming exit.

He veered over to the far-right lane. The steering was a lot harder now with no power coming from the motor, but he managed to make his exit. A traffic light was coming. The light was red and K-Dolla was coming in fast at 54 MPH. He tried the breaks and it slowed him a little, but the ABS (Automatic Braking System) wasn't working as well without the engine running. He was hoping the light would change by the time the car got to the intersection, but hope wasn't on his side. His speed was now at 27 MPH and traffic was at a standstill. To avoid running in the back of a city bus he swerved to the left then jumped the curve and hit a streetlamp to keep from hitting a daycare van full of children.

The front end of the Intrepid looked like a mangled ball of metal. K-Dolla's bloody head rested on the deployed airbag. He moaned in agony for the pain he felt. The impact of the airbag caused a two-inch gash on his temple. His ears were ringing, and he felt a pain in his neck. He could hear sirens in the distance.

His door swung open and a civilian in a motorcycle jacket came to assist him out of the car. "Hey man, are you okay?" K-Dolla could only make a groaning sound. The man helped him out of the car and laid him on the ground. K-Dolla looked at the time, he had four minutes left. He sat back up. His head was spinning. "Dude, you got to lie back down. That was some wreck you just had, the paramedics need to check you out, you might've seriously hurt something." K-Dolla pushed the man out his way and got to his feet. More people came over to help him. He pushed past them and jumped on the man's motorcycle. "Hey, that's my bike!" The man's words bounced off his back as he sped away.

The pipes of the Honda 900RR screamed as K-Dolla zoomed through the city streets. He turned onto Villard street and into a parking lot next to a pet store. He ran to the back door of the pet store and pounded on it. The door swung open, and he rushed inside. Out of breath, he protested to Cutthroat. "I'm here! I'm here!" Cîroc was sitting on top of a stack of Diamond dog food with Mac 11 in his lap while snacking on a box of Cheez-its. Victoria sat gagged and tied to a chair. She squirmed and cried as Wild-Child let a boa python crawl up her dress and between her legs. Cutthroat stood next to an enormous aquarium with an alligator inside it.

"You're three minutes late."

"Don't do this man. Do you know what I had to go through just to get here?"

"No, and don't give a fuck. Give me one good reason why I shouldn't feed that bitch to ole Cookie here?" Cutthroat held up a rat by its tail over the aquarium. The rat squeaked and squirmed. A second later, Cookie jumped out of the water and snatched the rat out of his hand. K-Dolla jumped back.

"Cut, I know where Billy Gunz is keeping your daughter. I did exactly what you told me to and found out. We can go there and get her back right now and you can keep the money instead of paying Billy." Victoria's eyes got big, and she muffled a louder scream. The snake had gotten closer than she liked. She could feel its head brushing against the crotch of her panties. "Come on Cut, please man."

"Wild-Child, put the snake back in its cage before he gave that a ho' an orgasm. Then tie that nigga K-Dolla back up and put both of them in the truck."

"But I did what you told me to do, why not just let us go and you'll never see or hear from us again."

"I said I would let y'all go when I'm finished with y'all. And until I get my daughter back, I'm not finished with neither one of you." Cutthroat looked over at Cîroc. "Cîroc let's roll." Cîroc hopped down from the stack of dog food and Cutthroat put his arm around him. "That was a gorgeous plan you came up with. Sending K-Dolla in seemed to really pay off. And your man the limo driver played his part well. It's thinking like that is what's going to get us where we going in this game."

"No doubt." Cutthroat slapped him on the back, and they loaded up headed to the old club 414 to get Pumpkin back. All Cutthroat could think was once he got her back, he was going to get the upper hand on Billy Gunz. It was time for big brother to put little brother in his place and teach him a lesson he wouldn't forget. Even if that meant little brother had to die to learn.

King Dream

Chapter 14

Pumpkin finished the last of her McDonald's fries and put the empty box into the bag. She picked up the McDonald's cup and took a sip of her Sprite. Cowboy's been keeping her fed with fast food and doing his best to keep her comfortable. He even brought down his small see-through flat-screen TV he brought home from the joint for her to watch. He figured as long as she was comfortable, she would keep quiet and not give him any trouble. But Pumpkin's been locked in the basement for two days and her patients were running thin. She was sick of taking birdbaths and being cramped in the small bathroom size room. The little cot she was being forced to sleep on was like sleeping on a bale of hay. Most of all she missed Cîroc. She needed him. She knew once he found out where Billy Gunz was hiding her, he would come and rescue her and anyone who had something to do with her kidnapping would have hell to pay from him and her father.

Then she thought, what if they never find out where he's keeping her and whatever deal they worked out, Billy Gunz double-crossed them and killed her? She had to come up with a plan. But coming up with a plan meant she had to think, focus, which was something she couldn't do right then and there. Her mind wouldn't let her. Her ass itched, her skin felt oily, and she hadn't shaved her pussy and legs in days. She never went this long without properly grooming herself and it was irritating her. She felt too dirty and needed a real bath to relax her mind and think clearly.

Cowboy had devised a system where she could reach him without yelling if she needed anything. He gave her an old Nextel flip phone with the keypad snatched out of it so she couldn't dial anyone. All she could do is chirp him through the walkie-talkie part of the phone.

She grabbed the Nextel and chirped him. "Tiki man." He wouldn't give her his name, so she started calling him Tiki man because of the mask he wore.

"What is it?"

"I need a bath."

"Use the sink."

"I'm tired of using the sink. I am a woman; I have certain needs that can't be attended to properly using a sink. I need a real bath!" She let go of the button and waited for him to chirp back. Ten seconds of radio silence went by. She chirped him again. "Hello? Did you hear me?" Still, nothing came back from the other end.

Pumpkin tossed the Nextel on the cot and plopped down next to it. She turned the TV to her favorite soap opera, *Bold and the Beautiful*. She watched the show and sipped on her Sprite trying to take her mind away from being trapped in the basement. That's how her father told her he did all that time in prison. He freed his mind every chance he could. He focused on different things and lived a lot in his imagination and future plans. Pumpkin felt if it worked good enough to get him through seventeen years it should work good enough for whatever little time she would be down there.

The *Bold and the Beautiful* show ended in a cliffhanger with Thomas hearing the voice of Hope coming from a closet. Just as he opened the closet the show ended. "Damn, I need to know if that was hope in the closet!" Pumpkin yelled at the TV. The sound of the deadbolt locks unlocking drew her attention to the door. The door opened and Cowboy walked in holding a black pillowcase. Pumpkin looked down at it. "What's that for?"

"You want a bath, right? Then you gonna have to wear this over your head while we travel through the house." He tossed it over to her. She stood up and put the pillowcase over her head. Cowboy came behind her and put a pair of furry white handcuffs on her wrist. The handcuffs were something he and his ex-girlfriend bought at Spencer's store inside the mall for their bedroom role-playing.

He marched her up the stairs then up another set of stairs that lead to the second level of the house. They walked down a hall to a room on the right. Cowboy closed the door behind them then removed the pillowcase from her overhead. Pumpkin looked around the room. The windows were boarded up. A doorway adjoined the bedroom with a bathroom. The door to the bathroom was removed. She knew that meant she wouldn't be having any privacy. Pumpkin looked at Cowboy and he pointed his head at the bathroom. She walked into the bathroom. Four strawberry-scented candles were lit and placed around the bathtub. A bubble bath was already prepared for her. Sitting on the toilet was a neatly folded, large, blue, dry towel, a pair of gray sweat pants, a white T-shirt, a pair of socks, panties, and a bra. A toothbrush, a tube of Colgate extra whitening, a washcloth, a bottle of Dove body wash, Secret deodorant, a razor, shaving cream, Cocoa butter lotion, and a bottle of cheap melon body spray. Cowboy had one of his hypes boost everything from the Family Dollar store up the way.

Cowboy laid back on the bed and turned the TV on. From where he was lying, he could see straight into the bathroom. Pumpkin took her shirt and pants off. There was no shower curtain for her to undress behind, so she wrapped the large towel over her body before removing her panties and bra. She dropped the washcloth into the tub and sat the razor, shaving cream and body wash down next to the tub. She dipped her toe in the water, it was nice and hot, just the way she liked it. Pumpkin got into the tub and took the towel off and held it out in front of her body like a shield until her body was completely submerged underwater. She dropped the towel on the floor and melted into the water.

Pumpkin laid soaking in the bathwater for ten minutes before moving a muscle. As she shaved her legs, she felt a pair of eyes on her. Through her peripheral, she could see Cowboy watching TV. At least he tried to make it seem that way, but Pumpkin could tell behind that mask he was really looking at her. To confirm her suspicion, she started to play with him a little. She grabbed the towel off the floor then propped herself up on the edge of the tub with her legs and thighs on full display and her intimate parts covered with the towel. Slowly she worked the razor up and down her legs and thighs while pretending not to notice the bath towel slipping off her breast. She could feel the towel sliding down and her areolas becoming exposed. Pumpkin could see Cowboy sneakily craning his neck anticipating the towel to drop a little lower so he could see her nipples. The towel was just about to expose her nipples when she gripped the towel and pulled it back over her breast. Cowboy threw his head back on the pillow. Pumpkin smirked, she could damn near hear the voice in his head screaming, *Damn*.

With her suspicions confirmed, Pumpkin now had a plan in mind. "Aye Tiki man."

"What?"

"If you don't mind, I would like to take my medicine now." Cowboy dug into his pocket and pulled out a bag of weed and a gram of coke. He reached down into his sock and retrieved a White Owl cigar. He walked over and handed it all to her. Pumpkin could see his eyes behind the mask, making a trail up her thighs, hoping to get a peek at what lies between them. "Um, thank you." Cowboy shook his head snapping out of his lustful daydream. He walked back into the room and laid back on the bed.

Pumpkin dropped the towel and sunk back down into the tub. She leaned over the tub to roll up her blunt. After breaking down the weed and putting it in the blunt she sprinkled the cocaine on top then rolled and sealed it with her lips. Pumpkin dried the blunt over one of the candles before sparking it up. She sucked in a deep pull of the primo smoke and leaned back in the tub.

With her foot, she turned on the hot water to arm the bath some more. Once the temperature was back right, she turned the water back off and smoked the blunt until it was down to it was a roach. Then she propped a leg up on the tub and began shaving her cat. When she was done, she put her hand down there and felt how smooth it now was. It felt so good she couldn't stop rubbing it. Her hand ventured from her pubic mound to her split. Her finger lightly rubbed against her clit and a moan escaped her mouth. The moan wasn't that loud, but it was loud enough that it caught Cowboy's attention and had him craning his neck once again. Her eyes appeared to be tightly closed but in reality, they were just tightly squinted. She could see everything Cowboy was doing.

She continued massaging her pussy. Using her other hand, she started massaging her breast. This time, because the bubbles had disappeared, Cowboy got a chance to see her nipples. He wanted to suck on them so bad he was biting his lip. Pumpkin grinded on her hand, throwing her head back twirling her hips, and allowing her moans to break noise barriers. Through squinted eyes, she could see Cowboy's pants rising with an erection. She wanted so badly to laugh at him, but she stayed in character as she pretended to bust a nut.

She leaned back in the tub a moment to catch her breath. Then she got out of the tub and dried off. Her back was to Cowboy and he could see her beautiful backside. It made him so hard he could've exploded in his pants then there. Pumpkin finished getting dressed then walked into the room and put the pillowcase over her head. "I'm ready." Cowboy cuffed her and marched her back downstairs.

Walking down the basement steps, she allowed her hand to bump against his dick. His dick pulsated at her touch. Cowboy walked her into her room, removed the handcuffs and pillowcase. Pumpkin looked behind her shoulders at him very seductively. "Thank you." Cowboy nodded his head. She switched her ass as she walked the short distance to the bed. She crawled onto the bed with her ass high in the air. Cowboy couldn't look anymore, or he was going to bust the zipper of his pants. He left out locking the door behind him. He leaned against the door and took his head.

"Billy, you better hurry up and get this girl before I fuck her, and she wouldn't want to leave." Cowboy went back upstairs to chill. Pumpkin had him right where she wanted him.

Pumpkin smoked the roach she had. Then fifteen minutes later she grabbed the Nextel and chirped Cowboy. "Aye Tiki man."

"What is it?"

"I need your help with something."

"What is it?"

"I think something's wrong with me. I get horny every time I smoke. Normally, Cîroc would fuck me good. If he wasn't around, I would play with myself. But this time no matter how many times I rub my pussy, I can't seem to satisfy myself. You think you could give me a hand or something a little longer and stiffer?" Cowboy didn't chirp back. The next thing she heard was him rushing down the basement steps. The deadbolt locks quickly unlocked, and the door swung open. Cowboy tried to retrieve the keys out of the lock, but Pumpkin was all over him before he could do anything. She pushed him against the door, lifted his shirt and kissed her way down. She squatted down, unbuckled his pants and pulled out his member. He was as hard as a brick. She spit on the head of it and massaged her warm, wet saliva up and down it. He licked his lips and looked down at her.

"Suck it, don't play with it. This mothafucka likes to be pleased not teased."

"Patience." Pumpkin held his nuts in her hand then opened her mouth wide. She took him deep down her throat until she reached the base of his dick. The sucking sounds she made turned him on and made his dick jump repeatedly inside her mouth. Her mouth moved swiftly up and down his shaft as she massaged his nuts. Cowboy pushed her head away.

"You got a wicked head game, baby. Let me see what that pussy do." Pumpkin got to her feet wiping her mouth with the back of her hand.

"Take your clothes off and give me a show. Then I'll do the same for you." Cowboy hesitated a second then said fuck it. He activated the Pandora app on his phone then tossed the phone on the cot. Lil Nas X's song, *Old Town Road*, played through the phone's speaker. Cowboy had no rhythm as he danced while unbuttoning his shirt and took it off then came his pants. Pumpkin covered her mouth to conceal her laughter. Cowboy had on a zebra-striped thong. He took them off.

"Your turn, baby."

"No problem." Pumpkin started to remove her sweatpants but stopped. "You know what, I ain't feeling this music."

"What you want to hear?"

"Play that *WAP* song by Cardi B and Megan Thee Stallion."

"Oh, you like that freaky music. I got you." He went over to the bed. His back was turned to her as he looked for her song. He stood wide-legged and that gave Pumpkin the opening she needed. With the grace of an NFL kicker, she ran over and kicked him as hard as she could in the nuts. He screamed from the top of his lungs. His mask came off as he fell to his hands and knees coughing and spitting. "You bitch!"

"I knew it was you, Cowboy. You know you're a dead man now." She ran out the door locking the deadbolt locks before he could get back to his feet. As she locked the last lock Cowboy started beating on the door.

"Open this door bitch!"

"I don't think so, bitch!" She ran up the steps and out the front door. She looked around and knew exactly where she was. She wasn't far from Ciroc's spot and that's where she was headed.

Chapter 15

After casing out the old 414 Club, Cutthroat decided it would be best to make their move later that night. Wild-Child stayed back at the pet store to babysit K-Dolla and Victoria. Cîroc went back to his spot to chill until Cutthroat called.

He sat back on the couch with his legs propped up on the coffee table watching an episode of Chicago PD. His eyelids were getting heavy. He'd been up for two days busting moves. He was about to doze off when his phone rang. It was an unknown number that showed up.

"Who this?"

"Tell me what you know about my father and how do you know it?"

"I had a feeling I would be hearing from you soon. But how did you get my number?"

"I have my ways. Now answer my question. What do you know about my father and how?"

"I heard this song the other day by this old rapper named Pastor Troy. It was called *Vice Versa*. He talks about what if everything we knew was right was really wrong. That would be mind-blowing, huh? That song reminded me of you."

"And why is that?"

"You smart as hell Pay Pay but you're blind as a fucking bat. Them niggas you fuck with ain't really who you think they are. Try opening up your eyes and you'll see the mothafuckas you call your friends are really your frenemies. You're on the wrong side of this war, bruh."

"If you want me to believe that then tell me what you know."

"Look, you got a lot of questions and I can't answer them all over the phone. If you really want answers then meet me at the old 414 Club at midnight tonight."

"How do I know you're not setting me up?"

"You don't." Cîroc ended the call then sent a text to another number. The text read:

He'll be there. Everything's working out just as you said it would...

A text came back that read:

Cool, get ready for one hell of a night, lil dog...

Cîroc put his phone away, clasping his hands behind his head, and leaned back on the couch. He closed his eyes and dozed off.

An hour and forty-five minutes later Cîroc awakened from his sleep by a loud banging at the back door. He jumped up from the couch. In one swift motion, he removed a .357 Magnum from the small of his back and cocked back the hammer.

He was home alone. Besides Wild-Child the rest of his crew was at the spot around the corner. He and his crew transferred all the traffic to the spot around the corner a few days ago. Every few months they move the spot's location to throw the police off. The house now was nothing more than a safe place Cîroc laid his head.

He walked cautiously through the house towards the back door. When he reached the kitchen, the back door became visible. The person on the other side was banging so hard the door was shaking. They tried turning the doorknob, but the door was locked and reinforced with a 2x4 board across it.

As quietly as he could Cîroc removed the 2x4 board from the door and unlocked it. Not even two seconds went by after he unlocked it did the door come flying open. Cîroc was an ounce of pressure away from pulling the trigger of the .357 magnum and sending a bullet through the head of the intruder. But when he saw who it was busting through the door, he lowered the gun and safely cocked it, releasing the tension on the hammer. Pumpkin ran into his arms. He wrapped his arms tight around her. "Baby, how did you, where were... Thank God you're home." He had so many questions but didn't what to ask them. All he wanted to do right then was hold her because that's she needed. All she did was cry and he could feel the tears streaming down her face and onto his neck.

Her tears dried up after two minutes of sobbing. She stepped back from his embrace and wiped her eyes and cheeks. She began telling him everything that happened, where she was being kept, and how she escaped. Cîroc was furious. "Grabbed that rope out the pantry drawer. We're going to go pay Cowboy a visit." Pumpkin did as she was told, and they left out headed over to Cowboy's house.

It took less than four minutes by car for them to get to Cowboy's house from his. When they arrived, the block was live, but everyone was too busy to notice them. At the end of the block, three little girls played Double Dutch on the sidewalk. A group of young boys played a game of hustle on a portable basketball hoop in the middle of the street. An old lady on the other side of the street in a floral pattern dress stood in front of her house watering her flowers.

Cîroc and Pumpkin got out of the car pulling their hoodies over their heads. Coming up the front steps Pumpkin could see the front door was still ajar like she left it when she ran out. It let her know Cowboy was still locked in the basement. They walked up the porch steps and drew their guns before walking inside, closing the door behind them.

Meanwhile down in the basement, Cowboy was walking around the room frantically in his underwear searching for a signal on his cellphone. He had to get a hold of Billy Gunz to inform him that Pumpkin escaped before she made it to Cîroc or Cutthroat. Little did he know he was too late. He stood on the bed with the phone held high. "Come on baby, give daddy just one bar." The deadbolt locks started to unlock, steering Cowboy's attention to the door. He waited for the door to open up but after thirty seconds of staring at it never did.

Cowboy slipped on his pants, walked over and pushed on the door. The door opened with ease. The basement appeared to be empty, there was no one in sight. A chair was placed in the middle of the basement. He walked cautiously through the basement knowing someone had to be there, that door didn't unlock itself.

He got to the stairs and jumped back in shock when he saw Pumpkin sitting at the top of the steps. "I thought yo ass would be miles away from here by now. I guess you just wanted to play with me, huh? What's the matter baby, sucking on this dick gave you Stockholm syndrome or something?" Cowboy laughed like a drunken hillbilly.

"Nah, I left. Then I came back so I could watch Cîroc kill you."

"What?" All the laughter and excitement left Cowboy's face. Before he could say another word Cîroc came from out of the shadows from behind him. The cold steel of his .357 Magnum barrel pressed against the back of Cowboy's skull. Cowboy froze in his tracks.

"Don't leave just yet. You and I need to have a conversation. I got a seat for you right over there." Cîroc pushed him away from the stairs and towards the chair in the middle of the basement. With his hands up, Cowboy proceeded towards the chair.

"Billy Gunz will be here any minute. I called him while I was locked in the room. If I were you, I would leave now." Cowboy was punk faking, hoping Cîroc would get scared and leave.

"If he were coming that would make my day. But we both know you couldn't make that call. I got the best cell phone service out here with the strongest signal and I'm not even getting any bars down here, so I know you bullshitting." Pumpkin pushed Cowboy and he fell onto the chair. Cîroc tossed his cowboy boots at his feet. He had grabbed them along with some other things from upstairs.

"Put those on. I watched enough western movies as a kid to know there's nothing a cowboy wants more than to die with his boots."

While Cowboy slipped his boots on Pumpkin untangled the rope to tie him down with. Cowboy slipped his fingers into a hidden pouch in his boots but couldn't find what he was looking for. "Looking for this." Cîroc held up Cowboy's switchblade knife. His heart dropped. That was his last line of defense. Though he was already outnumbered he felt the element of surprise would give him the advantage he needed to overpower Cîroc. Any hope of that happening was now gone.

Pumpkin tied his arms and legs tight to the chair. She stuffed a dirty sock into his mouth then sealed it in with a strip of duct tape.

"You got him tied down nice and tight, baby?" Pumpkin tugged on his binds showing there was no wiggle room.

"Tighter than a pair of jeans on Beyoncé." Cîroc held out his hand.

"Give me the pliers." Pumpkin retrieved the pliers from the back pocket of her jeans and handed them to him. "Since you want to be Billy Gunz errand boy you might as well be his messenger too. Tell him how I feel about people fucking with mines." Cowboy tried to mumble something through his gag that went unheard.

Cowboy's long fingernails became Ciroc's focus. He clamped the pliers down on his thumbnail and yanked it off. Cowboy's body squirmed; his head lifted to the ceiling. The veins in his neck became visible as he screamed a muffled scream through his gag from the top of his lungs.

Cîroc continued until all nine nails were sitting in a small bloody pile on the floor. Cowboy had tears in his eyes and was on the verge of passing out. But Cîroc wasn't finished with him just yet. He picked up a gas can he found in the basement and poured it all over Cowboy. He made a trail of gasoline that led from Cowboy to the basement stairs. He pulled a Zippo lighter from his pocket and held it out to Pumpkin. "You want to do the honors?"

"It would be my pleasure." She took the lighter, popped open the cover, and lit it. Cowboy mumbled and shook his head no with wide eyes. With a grimacing smile, Pumpkin dropped the lighter to the floor. "Oops!" The gasoline trail lit up with flames and swiftly made its way to Cowboy. He screamed and wiggled around in his chair as the flames engulfed him.

Cîroc and Pumpkin walked out of the house and back to their car. The block hadn't noticed a thing, everyone was still busy with the same activities they were when Pumpkin and Cîroc pulled up. "Pumpkin, I'm going to take you to a friend's house. I need you to lay low."

"No, I want to be with you, and I need to see my dad."

"Pumpkin, hear me out. It's just until later on tonight. Right now, we got the upper hand on Billy Gunz. Let us keep it that way. Okay?" Pumpkin got a cigarette out of the middle counsel and sparked it up.

"Okay. Just until later tonight?" Cîroc held up his pinky.

"I pinky swear." They locked pinkies then he kissed her pinky finger.

"Maybe I should get up out of here." Pumpkin pointed to the smoke coming out of the house. He started the car and they casually drove away.

Chapter 16

A six-foot metal fence with barbed wire lacing the top end surrounded the old 414 Club, making it only one way in and one way out. With their headlights off, Cutthroat, Cîroc along with Wild-Child and Big Vader drove the stolen Ford Expedition through the front gates. The club looked dark and deserted. They drove through the parking lot to the side door of the club then got out the truck.

Big Vader, a fat black Beanie Sigel looking brother with a bad breathing problem. They called him Big Vader because every time he moved, he wheezed and breathed so hard he sounded like Dark Vader.

Big Vader wobbled over to the door with an SK strapped on his shoulder. He pulled out a lock-picking kit and went to work. He was an expert at picking locks and cracking safes. In a matter of seconds, he had the door opened and they all were creeping inside with their guns out.

The side door had led to a hallway behind the VIP section. The hallway was used as an escape route for VIP guests in case the police came or someone started shooting up the club.

They walked into the VIP section. Though the club was vacant you couldn't tell it hadn't been used in years. The lights were dimly lit, Curtis Mayfield's song *Pusherman* played at mid-volume. Everything was kept in pristine condition. It was like the club never closed. But being there were no people around gave off an eerie vibe. "It's a lot of ground to cover in here. Everybody split up, put your phones on vibrate. If any of you finds her before me, hit my phone." They nodded their heads in agreement with Cutthroat then marched in separate directions.

Big Vader ventured off to behind the VIP bar. He picked up a bottle of liquor from the shelf. "Ace Of Spades! This that rich people shit here Jack. I got to try some of this." He looked around to make sure no one was looking. He smelled it then took a gulp. He made a sour face while looking at the bottle. "Umm-hmm, that's some good shit right there boy! I'm taking you with me." He slipped the bottle into the center pocket of his hoodie. He continued raiding the bar and all of a sudden, the air-conditioning blower came on. Something brushed past his shoes. Big Vader jumped back and looked down and saw two blue face hundred-dollar bills skating past his feet. "Ooh, where you come from?" He bent down, picked the bills up and stuffed them into his pocket. Two more bills came blowing by and he picked them up too. He looked to see where they were coming from. He rounded the corner of the bar and saw they were flying out of a cash box on the floor. He picked the box up and rummaged through the cash with a huge Chester's grin on his face. "It's a beautiful night tonight baby. Yes sir." A floorboard creaks behind. As he turned around a whisper from the barrel of a silencer sent a lead message straight between his eyes. Big Vader fell to the floor dead, still holding onto the cashbox. Joey Long stepped over Big Vader's dead body and continued his hunt for the rest of the crew.

Cutthroat and Cîroc walked through a door marked employees only. A blinking red light lit up the hall behind the door. The sounds of music began to fade the further they walked down the hall. "Keep your eyes peeled Cîroc. That damn Billy Gunz is a sneaky bastard."

"You ain't telling me nothing I don't know already, big dog. I'm just ready to take out Billy and his crew."

"And find Pumpkin, right?"

"Of course." Cîroc never told Cutthroat he had already found Pumpkin and got one of his peoples looking after her. He knew if Cutthroat knew he had Pumpkin already he wouldn't walk into Billy Gunz's trap. Cîroc needed him to walk into the trap so they could face off with Billy Gunz and the rest of the Order. He wanted to take the Order out of the game once and for all.

Cutthroat opened a door on the left side of the hall. Cîroc peered in from over his shoulder. Inside was a couch, mini-fridge, TV, a vanity mirror, and a coffee table. It was a greenroom for the entertainers that came to do shows at the club. "Nothing in here." Closing the door back they heard a woman's scream, which was quickly muffled, coming from towards the end of the hall. "That's Pumpkin!" Cutthroat moved swiftly down the hall towards the door the screams were coming from. Cîroc moved cautiously behind him, he knew Pumpkin wasn't in there and whatever was in there had to be a trap.

Cutthroat got to the door and slowly opened the door. The door led to a large stockroom filled with old bar furniture, cases of beer, and other liquor. The room was badly lit by the moonlight that came in from windows up high. Cîroc followed behind but kept his distance. More muffled screams for help came from a cooler further back in the room. The close sound of what he thought was Pumpkin's scream made Cutthroat recklessly sprint towards the cooler. The butt of a shotgun came out from behind a stack of Budweiser boxes. "Cut watch out!" It was too late. By the time Cutthroat saw it, the butt of the gun was being driven right into his face. He fell to the ground knocked out cold. Billy Gunz turned the shotgun around and trained it on Cutthroat. He kicked him to make sure he was out. Cîroc ducked off behind a stack of boxes and aimed his gun at Billy Gunz. Billy Gunz was unaware he was in Ciroc's crosshairs. Cîroc got ready to take the shot but felt the large cold barrel of a 30 Odd 6 on the back of his neck, then he heard Missy's voice.

"You squeeze, I squeeze. The difference is at this distance you can miss, I can't. So, drop the gun, or 2-2-3 shells are going to knock your head off your shoulders." Cîroc sat the gun down easy.

"That's a good boy. Now start walking." Cîroc complied. Billy Gunz and Joey Long were in front of them dragging Cutthroat's body by his arms. They stopped next to the area where the barstools were stored. Missy flipped a switch, and the lights came on. Using zip ties, Billy Gunz and Joey Long tied Cîroc and Cutthroat arms to the armrest and legs to the legs of the barstools they sat on.

Cutthroat was still out. Billy Gunz splashed him in the face with a bucket of ice water. He woke instantly yelling with the shock of the cold water splashing in his face. "Rise and shine big bro!" Cutthroat spit drips of water off his lips at Billy Gunz.

"Billy, I'm going to fucking kill you!" He tried to yank his arms loose from the armrest, but it didn't work. It only made the zip ties dig deeper into his skin. "Untie us and give me my daughter!"

"Pumpkin's not here."

"That's bullshit! I heard her screaming!"

"Oh, you mean this?" Joey Long pressed play on an iPod that was plugged into a speaker. A scream came out of the speaker followed by muffled screams. "That was some Hollywood sound effects. It's amazing the things you can download off the internet these days."

"Where's my daughter?"

"Where is my money? You thought I wasn't going to find out you turned K-Dolla against me? Nigga I knew the minute he walked into the meeting, he had traitor written all over him. To confirm my suspicion Missy here followed him from the meeting to the pet store where he met up with you. You used him to find out where we were hiding Pumpkin so you could come get her and not have to pay me or submit to the Order. I'm sure you probably kidnapped Victoria to get his sucka for love ass to turn on us. All's right so far?" Cutthroat mugged him with no reply. "I had your game plan all figured out, bruh." Billy Gunz shook his head at Cutthroat. "When will you stop underestimating me, Cut? I may be your little brother, but I'm the big dog in this game. And I ain't get this big by being stupid."

"What do you want Billy?"

"I told you, I want my money."

"You don't need it! Two hundred G's is nothing but lunch money to you!"

"Yeah, well I like to eat." Billy Gunz laughed at the same time he rubbed his stomach. "Why couldn't you just accept the position on the board and be satisfied?"

"Because I was supposed to rule the O-" Before he could finish his sentence, all the lights went out.

"Missy turn the lights on!"

"I'm trying Billy! Somehow the breaker box must've blown a fuse."

"Joey go turn it back on!"

"I don't know where the box is located!"

"It's on the east wall by the clutter of dartboard machines! Hurry up!" Joey rushed off to the breaker box.

A chuckle came from where Cîroc was sitting. "I know the big bad Billy Gunz ain't afraid of the dark, is he?" The moonlight gave off enough of a glow for Billy Gunz to see his punch land on the left side of Ciroc's jaw.

"Scared of the dark? Nah, but you should be scared of me being in the dark."

In Ciroc's direction, the moonlight didn't reach beyond his face. Behind him was so dark nothing or no one was visible to the naked eye. Billy Gunz turned around to face the area Joey Long walked off to. "Joey! Hurry up with the lights! I ain't got all day!" As Billy Gunz was yelling at Joey to get the lights on, and Missy was distracted flashing her phone light at Joey Long, Wild-Child had crept behind Cîroc.

"Shhh," he whispered to him then took the box cutter he was holding and cut the zip tie on his right hand off. Cîroc grabbed the box cutter from Wild-Child and quickly freed his left hand and legs. He picked up the barstool he was sitting in and clobbered Billy Gunz in the back with it. Missy focused the light of her phone at the scene of the commotion. She saw Billy Gunz fall to the floor unconscious. She went for the 30 Odd 6, but Cîroc already had Billy Gunz's Mossberg pump in his hand and had the drop on her.

"It seems the odds are on my side this time. You reach and I'll teach. And at this distance, I will blow your head off your shoulders before you could make another fingerprint on that riffle."

"Shit!" Missy held her hands up in defeat. The lights came on and a minute later Wild-Child was walking Joey long back over at gunpoint. Cîroc looked at Joey Long with a smile on his face.

"Ain't no fun when the rabbit got the gun, huh?"

"This ain't over."

"You're right. I'm gonna get you a Snickers because we've got a long night ahead of us." Joey Long looked at Missy and the look in her eye told him she was thinking the same thing. They were in for a long night of torture if they don't figure a way out and figure one out real soon.

Chapter 17

Cîroc checked a text as Wild-Child finished tying everybody up. He had everyone lined up next to each other zip-tied to barstools. "Cîroc! Wild-Child! Get over here and cut me loose from these zip ties." Wild-Child went to get the box cutter off a stack of boxes where Cîroc was standing with his face in his phone texting. As soon as he reached for the box cutter, Cîroc grabbed his wrist.

"What you doing?"

"I'm finna cut the O'G loose."

"Nah, he good."

"What the fuck you mean I'm good? Get y'all ass over here and untie me!" Cîroc put his phone away and walked towards Cut-throat.

"See that's what I'm talking about Cut, you too hostile right now. We got some company coming to join the party and I can't trust you to be on your best behavior when you get like this. Trust me it's better this way."

"Cîroc you get me out of this chair right now!" Cîroc walked away from him. "Wild-Child, cut me loose!"

"Sorry O'G, but my loyalty is to Cîroc."

"You little punk ass bitches. How dare you cross me? Me, the nigga that put y'all piss po asses on?" Billy Gunz laughed as he began to gain consciousness.

"Now ain't that about a bitch. Can't trust no mothafucka these days, huh big bruh." Billy Gunz laughed even louder at him.

"Go fuck yourself, Billy." A door out in the hall could be heard opening. Cîroc looked at Wild-Child.

"That must be Big Vader. His services are no longer needed. Go take care of him." Joey Long looked at Billy Gunz and whispered to him.

"That definitely ain't Big Vader." Billy Gunz knew that meant Joey Long had already offed Big Vader. It was the only way Joey Long could be that sure it wasn't him.

"I'm on it." Wild-Child jogged off in the direction of the hallway.

Billy Gunz had to make a move, he called Cîroc over to him. "Since it's obvious things aren't working out with you working under Cutthroat, how about you be a playa and untie me and we'll put those hustling skills of yours under new management. Give you a position that'll have you living like a boss. You know I've been having my eye on you for quite some time."

"Is that right?"

"No bullshit. I see you got a lot of hustle in you. You a little wild but we can tame that down some. Let me tell you what I would do for you. I'll give you half a brick for every two bricks you off for me. With the way you hustle, you could easily off twelve bricks a week. That's some serious money for yo ass. I'm telling you, fuck with me and you'll eat good." Cîroc put on a thinking face. Billy Gunz couldn't help but show his cockiness by smirking. To see Cîroc debating his offer in his mind gave him even more confidence in winning him over. But the joke was on Billy Gunz. Cîroc shook his head declining his offer.

"Nah, I'm good. I don't need your money B, I got plenty of that."

"If you ain't doing this for the money then what's yo angle lil dog?"

"Yeah, that's what I want to know." Cutthroat agreed. Cîroc ignored their question and walked over to where Missy was sitting. He had noticed she was slipping out of one of her zip ties.

"And what you think you're doing?" She tried moving faster to free her hand. Cîroc grabbed her arm to stop her.

"Let me go!" He smacked her across the face, she let out a brief scream.

"Shut the fuck up and be still."

"I know you didn't just smack my bitch. You is a real disrespectful lil mothafucka ain't you?" Cîroc tightened the zip-ties on her wrist so tight they made indentions on her wrist. Then one by one duck taped everyone's mouth except Billy Gunz. As he did so he heard footsteps behind him. Without looking he already knew who it was. "Wild-Child next time make sure you tighten the zip ties. This bitch almost got loose." He didn't get a response. When he turned around Wild-Child was standing there frozen. "Did you hear what I said?" Pay Pay, with his gun to Wild-Child's head, stepped from behind him. Cîroc raised his pistol and aimed it at Pay Pay.

"Wild-Child's a little speechless right now, but I'm sure he heard you. Ain't that right Wild-Child?" Wild-Child nodded his head. Cîroc checked the time on his phone, it was 11:27.

"You a little early, aren't you? I wasn't expecting you for another thirty-three minutes."

"I thought I'd show up early to get the lay of the land." Pay Pay's eyes scanned the room. "It's a good thing I did because it seems like you got quite the surprise party going on here."

"Pay Pay, thank God you're here my nigga. Pop them lil niggas and untie us." Pay Pay pointed his gun at Cîroc but kept ahold of Wild-Child by his collar.

"Oh my god, shut the fuck up! You talk too much Billy G." Cîroc put a strip of duct tape over his mouth.

"Untie them."

"I can't do that one fam."

"Oh, you going to do it or I'm going to blow your fucking head off."

"Look you came here for answers, right?" Pay Pay didn't respond. "I take your silence as a yes. Allow me to keep my word and give you the answers you came for. And if you still want me to cut your friends loose, I will. But I doubt you would kill me."

"And what would make you believe something that stupid?"

"Because blood is thicker than mud."

"What the fuck is you saying?"

"He's saying he's your brother," a voice coming down one of the liquor aisles said. The boxes of booze hid the man's image from everyone's view. More than two sets of footsteps could be heard headed towards the party. Pay Pay ping-ponged his aim between Cîroc and the area where the footsteps were coming from. K-Dolla was the first to come into view followed by Victoria and Pumpkin. All three had their hands tied together in front of them and their mouths gagged. A man wearing a Derby hat and a gray Tom Ford suit came in behind them holding an AK-47.

Pay Pay got a look at the man's face and knew who he was. It was no mistake by the look of shock on their faces that the rest of the Order knew who he was too.

"Martin? You're my cousin Martin."

"You remember me?"

"Only from a photo. But what are you doing here and what do you mean Ciroc's my brother?"

"I'm here for justice and truth. Uncle Bobby is Ciroc's father too. I'm going to explain everything in a minute. First, I need to get these people tied down to those barstools."

Cîroc and Wild-Child tied down Pumpkin, Victoria, and K-Dolla. They were lined up side by side in the following order from left to right, Victoria, K-Dolla, Joey Long, Missy, Pumpkin, Cutthroat, and then Billy Gunz. Pay Pay had so many questions and until they got answered, he didn't know who to trust. For that reason, he kept his gun and an eagle eye on everybody.

"Alright, time to get down to business," Martin said as he pulled up a barstool and took a seat in front of everyone. "Dig these blues, Pay Pay. To understand what's going on right now you need to first understand the past. My Uncle Bobby, your father, was the biggest drug lord in the country. He used to move his dope on Wonder Bread trucks, that's how he got the name the Bread-Man. Joey Long, Missy, K-Dolla, Cutthroat, and Billy Gunz all worked for the Bread-Man. He took them all under his wings when they weren't shit but dusty ass kids hustling stolen cassette tapes just to get a bag of weed, some Mad Dog 2020, and a pack of cigarettes. They were like his kids. His greedy lil kids that no matter how much he fed them, they always wanted more. Ain't that right, Billy?" Billy Gunz jerked around in his chair and mumbled a fuck you to Martin.

Pay Pay looked over at Cîroc who was pulling a bottle of Bailey's Irish Cream out of one of the boxes. He opened the bottle and turned it up.

"How is he, my brother?" Cîroc wiped his mouth with the back of his hand.

"I could tell you that story, big bro. I know it like the back of my hand. I used to have my mama tell it to me almost every night as a bedtime story when I was a shorty. It went like this...

It was a rainy day in May. My mother, Bella, was working her normal first shift at George Webb's Diner on Oakland Avenue. The Bread-Man was a regular there. Out of all the times he came there, he and Bella never conversed about anything more than him giving her his order and her taking it down. It was the same routine every time. He would come in take a seat at a booth in the middle of the restaurant with a window view. Then he would order a cup of black coffee, eggs with cheese, and bacon on toasted bread with strawberry jelly. He would read the paper as he ate and when he left, he would always leave a twenty-dollar tip for Bella.

This particular day, things went a little different. He took a seat at his regular booth and ordered his usual. Bella noticed something was off, not with the Bread-Man, but with a man seated at the counter. The man didn't look too friendly, and he kept an evil eye on the Bread-Man. Bella had a bad feeling in her gut. That bad feeling made her watch him just as hard as he was watching the Bread-Man.

The Bread-Man was seated with his back to the man at the counter. He was reading his paper and sipping his coffee. Bella was pouring coffee for a white couple seated in the booth directly behind the Bread-Man. From the corner of her eye, she watched as the man at the counter put his hand inside his leather trench coat. She saw his hand wrap around the wooden handle of a gun. He didn't pull it out, yet he kept his hand posted on it. He looked around the restaurant then got up and walked towards the Bread-Man with his hand still inside his coat. His eyes were locked on him. The bad feeling in Bella's stomach grew stronger. The Bread-Man couldn't see him coming. For some unknown reason to her, she had a powerful urge to do something. As the man got ready to pass the table she was standing at, she did the only thing she could think to do. She pretended to trip over something.

SPLASH!!

The man screamed from the top of his lungs as the coffee flew out of the coffee pot and into his clean-shaven face. He fell to the floor rolling around and clawing at his face. "I'm so sorry! I must've tripped over something." Bella tried to nurse the man's wounds with a towel that was clipped to her apron. Others in the restaurant came close to see how they could help.

"Get the hell away from me!" The man yelled and pushed her away. He got to his feet and pulled out his gun, waving it around the diner. People in the diner gasped and stepped away from him.

He had second-degree burns all over his face and his skin was peeling. He went over the booth the Bread-Man was sitting at, but the Bread-Man had disappeared. "God Damn it!" The man ran out of the diner in search of him.

The manager at George Web knew that type of man wouldn't sue but he was afraid the man might come back and harm Bella for messing up his face. For that reason, he fired her.

Bella came back to the diner that Friday to pick up her last check and into the Bread-Man on the way out. He offered her a ride home and she accepted. In the car, he thanked her for what she did then made her an offer she dared not to refuse. He told her how he was an important person and needed a decoy personal life to protect his family. He told her if she agreed to do it, she wouldn't need for shit for the rest of her life. She was game for it. The next day he had some movers come to her mother's house and move her into a nice condo on the south side of town. Though she never really asked him for anything, he gave her everything. Not because he loved her, but to keep up the illusion. It wouldn't look right if she was supposed to be the woman of one of the greatest drug lords and not have the finest things and the best of everything.

Bella, after a while, grew feelings for the Bread-Man and he had started to grow feelings for her too. Play that type of role with a person long enough it's bound to happen. But his feelings could never be as strong as they were for Resa and they both knew that.

A day before The Bread-Man took that last trip out of town that led to his death, Bella told him that she was pregnant. He was happy but worried about how Resa would feel to know he let things get that deep between him and Bella. They both knew it would hurt her. Though he told Bella he would have to tell her when he got back from his trip. He said it was the right thing to do. But The Bread-Man never returned alive.

And that's the story of my great conception."

"I could've told it better, lil cuz. Now, let's find out if our friend K-Dolla could tell his part of the story just as good and honest as you." K-Dolla shook his head no. But it didn't matter if he told it or not, the truth was coming out and it was nothing that he could do about it.

Chapter 18

Martin removed the gag from K-Dolla's mouth. "Alright Dolla, it's yo time to shine baby. Let's hear it." K-Dolla turned his head away from him.

"I ain't got nothing to say."

"Sure, you do. Tell us about that proposition Javier offered you and what happened with it. Or do you need a little encouragement? Wild-Child, cut Victoria loose and bring her here." With the box cutter in hand, Wild-Child went over to Victoria and cut her loose then walked over to Martin.

"Leave her alone!" Martin passed Cîroc his AK-47 then pulled out a nickel-plated Desert Eagle from his suits inside jacket pocket. He snatched Victoria and put the gun to the side of her head.

"You motivated now, preacher?"

"Okay, I'll talk," K-Dolla said in a low tone.

"I can't hear you, what you say?" Martin cocked the gun back then put it back to the side of her head. Victoria screamed through her gag.

"I'll talk! I'll talk! Just please stop pointing that gun at her." Martin took a seat and made her sit on the floor in front of his barstool. He sat the gun down on his lap.

Alright, the floor is yours." K-Dolla looked over at Joey Long and Billy Gunz. They both were shaking their heads no and mumbling through their mouth gags trying to get him to keep quiet. K-Dolla turned his head to a scared Victoria who sat on the floor shaking with tears in her eyes. The look on her face was enough for him to confess his darkest secrets to anyone. And that's just what he began to do...

"After Javier caught me and Victoria, he had me meet him downstairs in the hotel's bar. We sat at a table inside the bar, just the two of us. Javier ordered shots of tequila for us and gave me a

lot of small talks while puffing on one of those funky-ass Garcia Vega cigars. I told him to cut the small talk and tell me about the proposition he had for me. He grinned showing off his two gold fangs. He said to me, "Okay, here's the deal amigo. I'm going to give you my daughter's hand in marriage and make you a very wealthy man. In exchange, you're going to take out Carlito." I was hoping he wasn't asking what I thought he was asking of me. I had to clarify what he meant. So, I made him explain.

"What exactly do you mean by taking him out?" He blew out a trail of smoke then answered my question.

"You know exactly what I meant, Kevin. Kill him." I held my hands up.

"Whoa, whoa, whoa! You want me to kill Carlito? What the hell you think the Bread-Man would do to me if he found out I killed his supplier?"

"Don't worry about the Bread-Man. I have a feeling that wouldn't be much of a concern for him."

"Why wouldn't it? If something happens to Carlito, the Columbians will hold the Bread-Man responsible." Javier had got up from the table and put his arm around me.

"Don't concern yourself with those matters. How can you save another man's head from the sword when yours is under the guillotine? You got until tomorrow night to have it done or you'll be the one that's dead. Tell Victoria I said goodnight. You kids have fun, I'm going to get another room for myself." He put his cigar out in my drink and left.

I sat there in the bar for another hour or so wondering what I should do. I couldn't kill the largest drug lord in South America and expect to live and talk about it. I thought about how I couldn't betray the Bread-Man like that either. I hadn't known him as long as the rest of the crew, but he was still like a father to me. I weighed all those things in my head and made up my mind that Javier would have to kill me because I wasn't going to do it.

I got up and walked back to the room. When I went inside Victoria was asleep. She looked so beautiful lying there in her silk Prada pajamas. I took off my clothes and crawled into bed with her. I wrapped my arms around her desiring to hold her as close to me as I possibly could for one last night. I kissed her neck, and not meant to awaken her. She turned over, smiled and kissed me on the lips. Her sweet lips were like honey on mines. I couldn't take my lips off hers. We kissed and made love until the sky glowed orange with the shine of the rising sun. Then we laid there in each other's arms confessing our love for one another. It was then my mind had changed. I was going to do whatever it took to have her in my life forever. Even if that meant killing Carlito and betraying the Bread-Man.

I got out of bed later that day. My window of getting close to Carlito without anyone knowing was small. Because of that, I had to time everything down to the second. Carlito had a ritual he did each time he came to Corpus Christi. The day everyone leaves Texas and goes home, which is normally after a few days of partying, be the day Carlito and the Bread-Man do business. On that day Carlito always stopped at a nearby Catholic church to say a quick prayer. It was the only time his goons had orders to leave his side. His prayers were quick, no more than four minutes and he would be back out the church doors. That's why perfect timing was everything.

I jumped in the shower and got dressed. Victoria had ordered us room service. It was steak, eggs, bagels, grits, and freshly squeezed orange juice. It all looked and smelled delicious, but I couldn't eat. I didn't have an appetite. I gave her a kiss and left out.

I got to the church twenty minutes before Carlito showed up. The church was empty except for the priest lighting candles at the altar. I crept up behind him and whispered in his ear. "Don't turn around father. I need a favor from you."

"And what is that my son?"

"I need you to go off somewhere and pray for me for the next half hour. If you could do that for me, I would love to make this generous donation to the church." I reached past him and laid ten-grand in cash on the altar in front of him. The priest looked at the money for a moment. Then he made the symbol of the cross across his chest and pocketed the money.

"You will be in my prayers, my son." The priest left the main area of the church and went through a door and disappeared into another corridor of the church.

I heard Pablo and Gordo, two of Carlito's men, talking in Spanish to each other about how they searched every inch of the church except the priest's side of the confession booth before Carlito came in to pray. They argued about it being disrespectful and bad luck to do so. Then Gordo went into this long story about how a friend of his when he was a kid went into the priest's side of the confession booth to play around and got killed by a stray bullet that night. That being said, I hid in that part of the confession booth.

Like clockwork, twenty minutes later Gordo and Pablo were walking into the church to inspect it. I watched them through the vented holes in the Booth's door. Once they were satisfied it was safe, they walked out and Carlito walked in. He walked up to the altar and lit one of the candles then made a cross across the chest and got down on his knees. It was showtime. I crept out of the booth and began making my way towards him.

Now, I have lied before, stole, and even cheated people, but before that day I had never killed anyone. My hands shook badly. I was so nervous. My stomach was going haywire. I thought I was going to throw up my empty gut. Even though it would've been a lot easier than what I resulted to, I couldn't shoot him. I couldn't pick up a silencer on such short notice. So, to increase my chances of making it out of there alive, I had to find another way of offing him.

The priest's stole was laid out on one of the pews. I picked it up and wound it up until it was like a rope in my hands. I snuck up behind him and wrapped it around his neck. He was still on his knees and trying to get to his feet, but I had my weight resting on his back. He clawed at my hands and made choking noises. I kept pulling and squeezing tighter. He tried to reach for his gun but passed out before he could get to it.

It was too much work trying to strangle him, that shit was taking longer than I expected for him to die that way. While he was passed out, I placed his chin on the altar's step then stumped my foot down as hard as I could on the back of his neck. It made a snapping sound and judging by the way his head was laying loosely on his back it was no doubt he was dead. I dipped out the back door as fast as I could and went back to the hotel on time to ride out to the meeting with the rest of the crew...

"There's my story, the big secret I held deep. All I can say, Pay Pay, is that I'm sorry." Martin stood up then yanked Victoria up off the floor and put the gun to her head.

"You sorry? Nigga, you betrayed one of the realest niggas ever for a bitch. You didn't even do it for the money, the money was just icing on the cake for you. You sold out for a once-a-month bleeding ass bitch. A bitch who set you up and never really gave a fuck about you."

"That's a lie, Victoria loves me just as much as I love her!"

"You is a dumb mothafucka. I guess I'm going to have to break the game down for you. Javier wanted to take over the drug game in Columbia, but he had to first get rid of Carlito. He couldn't do it himself without signing his own death warrant. He found out you and Victoria were messing around long before he caught y'all at the hotel. He came up with his plan way back then and he was just waiting for the right moment to execute it. When he found out Carlito was bringing the Bread-Man three times his normal order, he saw no better time to execute his plan than then.

His plan was to first play on Victoria's emotions. He told her to make you prove you loved her by allowing him to catch the two of you together and give you an ultimatum to marry her or take some cash to leave her alone. But we all now know that wasn't the ultimatum he gave you; it was just what he needed Victoria to believe to go along with his plan. When she found out the truth, she was pissed. She tried to warn me, but it was too late."

"Why would she try and warn you?"

"You still don't get it, huh?" Martin removed Victoria's gag then kissed her passionately. K-Dolla's eyes went wide, and you could damn near see steam coming from his head. "Victoria's my bitch and always has been. It was me who told her to fuck with you to keep away the suspicion of me and her being together. And most of all because I never trusted you or the rest of The Order. Victoria stayed with you to keep a spy's eye on The Order. She constantly kept me updated on what was going on, that's how I was able to stay ten steps ahead of you niggas. I knew exactly how y'all was moving. Every Wednesday and Saturday where do you think she disappears from seven in the morning until after ten-thirty at night? I'll answer that for you. She's with me." K-Dolla tried to bust out the chair.

"Lies! You a god damn lie, Martin." Martin exhaled and shook his head at the shame K-Dolla was displaying.

"I guess that old saying is true, love is blind." Martin passed the Desert Eagle to Victoria. "Vicky baby, show this nigga where your heart is." Victoria walked over to K-Dolla.

"Victoria, say it ain't so. You love me, right? You're my wife, we made vows." She bent down and kissed him on the lips.

"We did baby. I said 'til death do us part. And I meant that." She swiftly raised the gun and *BOOM!!* A bullet went through his forehead splattering brain matter all over the boxes behind him. His body slid out of the chair and fell to the floor. His lifeless eyes were wide open, but K-Dolla was no more.

King Dream

Chapter 19

Even after seeing the gun in her hand, it still took him by surprise to see Victoria shoot K-Dolla. The man he thought she was head over hills for now laid dead on the floor by her own hand. Pay Pay's mind was on a rollercoaster ride. His head was spinning out of control with the things he was hearing. He couldn't believe how deep this shit was getting.

"I'm sorry everyone, but I had to get the softest nigga in the room out the way first. He was killing my vibe." Martin skipped over Joey Long and approached Missy. He walked circles around her as he spoke. "You, Missy, have always been quite the liar. But there will be none of that today. Because what we have here today is the table of truth. Though it's not literally a table in front of you, we shall pretend that it is. And at this table of truth, you are not allowed to tell not even the smallest lie. If you do, there will be dire consequences, and I do mean dire." He cut Missy free and took off her gag.

"Thus said, I want you to put your left hand on the invisible table, your right hand across your heart, and repeat after me. I, Missy Ann Carter, swear to tell the truth, the whole truth and nothing but the truth so help me God."

Missy put her left hand on the invisible table and her right one over her heart and repeated everything he said with tears in her eyes and a tremble in her voice. "Good girl. What I want you to do is tell us all about trailer park Missy, and how you met the Bread-Man."

Missy shut her eyes and lowered her head. Martin put his hand under her chin and lifted her head back up. "Missy, the truth shall set you free. Tell it or die." Missy wiped away the tears that threatened to fall from her eyes and began her story...

King Dream

I was raised in a small trailer park on the south side of Milwaukee. My mother, Rachel, and stepfather, Tyler, were heroin addicts. I never knew my real father. We were dirt poor, my mom and stepfather sold everything we had to get high.

When I was about thirteen years old, my mother and Tyler were jonesing real bad for a fix. Normally, my mother would go out prostituting, but this day she was too sick to move. Even my stepfather's beatings couldn't get her to hit the track. Tyler needed his fix and money to get to the temp services the next day, so he talked my mother into making me hit the track. He told her that I would bring them much more money than she was bringing in every night. He had her picture all of the drugs and other things they could buy if she sent me out there. My mother was immediately sold on the idea. She didn't even put up a fight. She made me get all dolled up in makeup and a dress that was so short my butt cheeks hung out. Tyler took me to the hoe scroll on National Street. He gave me orders on what to do. I wasn't on the track more than three minutes before a car came to pick me up. Twelve minutes and fifty bucks later, I had lost my virginity to a Mexican trick. I brought the money back to Tyler who was sitting in the truck. All he said was to get back to work and earn my keep, then he pulled off leaving me to hustle my sore ass some more.

I had screwed four more tricks since Tyler left and I was hungry. I walked to a nearby Pick'n Save grocery store. I bought a whole roasted chicken and a peach Faygo soda pop. I walked to a bus stop just outside the grocery store, sat down, and ate. I hadn't eaten in two days and that chicken tasted like a five-star meal. A bus arrived as I was eating. Groups of people exited the bus. I had chicken grease all over my face and hands and no napkin. I was looking for something to wipe my hands and face off with when two young black guys approached me.

One of the boys said, "Damn snowflake that chicken smells good as ever right now." He introduced himself as Billy Gunz and his friend as Joey Long. He then offered to smoke a blunt with me if I shared my chicken with them, so I did. The three of us conversed and blew a blunt of some dirt weed that gave us a twenty-minute high. After we smoked and ate, we parted ways. They were cool. We continued our ritual of meeting up at the bus stop to smoke and eat. Over the next couple of months, the three of us had gotten close. They were my escape from life at home and I enjoyed every second of being with them.

On this one particular day Billy's brother, Cutthroat, had just got out of juvenile detention for stealing cars. It was my first time meeting him. We were at our normal hangout; Cutthroat was in the grocery store getting sodas. We put another blunt in rotation while we waited on him so we could eat. Just as I passed the blunt to Joey, Tyler's truck came to a screeching stop in front of us. He got out of the truck and rushed over to me, snatching me to my feet and slammed me against the wall of the bus shelter.

"Why aren't you out here working like you supposed to? Are you trying to keep me and your mother sick?" I tried to explain to him that that wasn't the case I was just hungry. But Tyler was jonesing too bad to listen. He kept pushing me against the wall causing me to bang my head against the plexiglass bus shelter.

Billy Gunz yelled at him to leave me alone, but he didn't listen. All of a sudden, Cutthroat came out of nowhere putting Tyler in the headlock. Billy Gunz picked up a stick and started beating Tyler with it. Tyler finally let go of me, Billy Gunz pushed me out the way. Tyler ran out of the fight, so Cutthroat released his hold and he fell to his knees gasping for air. Billy Gunz kicked him in the stomach. Tyler puked and fell over on his back. Cutthroat put his foot on Tyler's neck cutting off his air supply. Then he told him if he ever fucked with me again, he would kill him. Then we ran off.

King Dream

I stayed with Billy and them for almost a month. During that time, they taught me a lot about the streets. Being a white girl, I was able to help them pull off many scams and hustles. One of our hustles was robbing tricks. I was a decoy for them. I would pick up Johns on the hoe stroll and have them park at a certain location. It was a dead-end alley with a bunch of bushes and shrubs at the end of it. As soon as the john would pull down his pants the boys would come out of the bushes with these realistic-looking BB guns. Once they had their guns on him, I would take off. Then they would make the john give them his pants with his wallet in it and run off.

This one time we tried to pull that hustle shit didn't go so well. This local hustler name Frog rolled up on me flashing a bankroll. The boys were posted in the bushes waiting for me to bring my next target their way. I got in the car and gave him directions on where to go, but he told me he had somewhere else in mind. He drove to a parking lot behind these apartments on 3rd and Mitchell Street. He pulled out his bankroll and peeled me off a hundred bucks then put the bankroll back in the right pocket of his leather jacket. He had the handle of a revolver sticking out of his left pants pocket. Even that didn't deter me. By all means, I had to have that bankroll.

Frog pulled his cock out and told me to give him some head. I complied. I looked up at him while I was handling my business and saw that his head was tilted back, and his eyes were closed. I crept my hand into his jacket pocket. I had my hand wrapped around the money and slowly began to retract it from his pocket. He started to lift his head. I just sucked him faster to distract him. When I did that his head fell back on the headrest and he closed his eyes. I went back to work trying to get the money out of his pocket. I was starting to taste his pre-cum and knew he was going to bust soon, so I had to move faster.

I got the money halfway out, but my movement was too clumsy, and I startled him. He looked down and caught my hand in his pocket. "Bitch, you trying to steal from me!" I reached for the door and got it open. He grabbed me before I could get out. I did the only thing I could think to do, I screamed rape.

It was this man who was coming out of one of the apartments and going to his car that heard my cry. The man and I made eye contact and he could see that I was a kid. I told him to help me because this man kidnapped me and was trying to rape me. Without thinking twice, he came to my rescue. He told Frog to let me go. Frog flashed his gun and told him to mind his own business. The man held up his hands and backed away. I thought the man was going to run off and I was going to be done for. The next thing I heard and saw was four shots ripping through Frog's chest. Frog fell face forward onto the car's horn. The man pulled me out of the car and made sure I was okay.

After sorting things out with the police, I was forced to go back to the custody of my mother. The man told me his name was Bobby. My reluctance to want to go back to my mother's house must've told him something wasn't right at home because he slipped me his pager number and told me if I ever needed anything to hit him up.

It wasn't even a whole two weeks that went by before I found myself having to use that number. My mom and Tyler were back to trying to force me into prostituting. I wasn't trying to hear it. I wasn't going to sell myself anymore. Tyler snapped and beat the snot out of me. I ran to a neighbor's house and paged Bobby, 911. He called back ASAP. I told him what happened and thirty minutes later he was at the trailer park. He walked me back over to my mother's trailer. I thought he was going to kick Tyler's ass or kill him. Instead, he sat my mom and Tyler down and asked how much it was going to cost him for my mother to sign custody over to him. They told him two-grand. That's all I was worth to them. Bobby gave them five to do it right then and there. I went wide-eyed to see him drop so much bread on the table for my poor white ass.

He leaned over and whispered to me, "Don't look so surprised, baby girl. You're worth way more than any man could afford. It's just sad that they don't know that." I could've cried at how special he made me feel at that moment. Things could only get greater for there.

And things did. Bobby gave me my own apartment, taught me how to drive and bought me a car, set me up in school, and taught me the dope game. Life was great. I was getting money and didn't want for nothing. Bobby was the father I never had.

But I didn't forget about the boys. Once I got fully settled in my new life, I introduced them to Bobby. Cutthroat had gone back to juvenile detention at the time for violating his probation and catching another case. Meanwhile, the four of us became like family. Bobby taught Joey and Billy the dope game also. He took a real shine to Billy. He said Billy was made for this game. Billy soon became his right-hand man and Bobby taught him everything he knew about the dope game. We all hustled hard and was never broke a day in our lives. That's my story...

"That's a hell of a story. A sad past you had there, Missy. It's a good thing you had my Uncle Bobby there to give you a better life. It's a shame how you and the rest of your crew repaid him though. And to put you on game about something else, that man, Frog, that Uncle Bobby killed for you, it was his brother that tried to kill Uncle Bobby that day at George Webs. Your lie almost cost my uncle his life that day. And it could've cost Bella hers." Martin pointed his gun at her as he talked.

"Please, don't, don't kill me. I was just a foolish little girl that didn't know better."

"I'm not the judge and jury on that. I'm not the one who's going to decide who lives or dies tonight. That responsibility is in the hands of Pay Pay and Cîroc. I gathered them here tonight to judge the hands that hold the blood of their father on them." Martin looked at Pay Pay and Cîroc. "What do y'all say, boys? Does Missy live or dies?" Cîroc pointed his gun at her face.

"I say we kill this bitch!"

"No!!" Missy screamed. Pay Pay put his hand on top of Ciroc's gun making him lower it.

"Hold tight a moment. I want to see how this whole story plays out first. After I hear what everyone has to say, then we can decide what to do with them."

"That's cool with me." Cîroc put his gun in his waist and turned the bottle of Bailey's Irish cream back up.

Missy could only hope that she had done more right than wrong in Pay Pay's and Ciroc's eyes. If not, she was sure there would be some bullets with her name on them.

King Dream

Chapter 20

Martin circled their barstools like a shark that circles its prey. He stopped in front of Cutthroat and snatched the duct tape off his mouth. "It looks like it's your turn Cut." Martin dug into the pocket of Cutthroat's hoodie.

"What the fuck is doing?"

"Relax. You looked like you could use a smoke." Martin took a lighter and pack of cigarettes out Cutthroat's pocket. He lit a smoke for him then placed it between his lips. The tip of the cigarette glowed a fiery red as he took a hard pull of it. It was exactly what he needed to relax his nerves before going into his part of the story.

"How about a long swallow of that bottle of Hennessey before I start talking." Martin nodded his head at Wild-Child. Wild-Child retrieved a fifth of Hennessy out of one of the liquor boxes. He opened the bottle and put it to Cutthroat's lips. He drank a quarter of the bottle without stopping. Wild-Child put his cigarette back between his lips. Then Cutthroat began his story...

Like Missy said, I was in the joint when they originally met the Bread-Man. When I got out everything had changed. My little brother was having more money than I ever had. He was running the crew like a real boss. He even put me on.

Billy introduced me to the Bread-Man a few weeks after I touched down. We met up with him at a dice game at the Diamond Inn motel. He was smoking a joint and rolling the dice when we walked in. The first person he noticed was Missy. "Hey, there goes daddy's baby girl!" Missy walked over to him.

"Hey, dad." Then gave him a kiss on the cheek.

"Kiss the dice and give your old man some good luck." She kissed the dice. The Bread-Man shook them then shot the dice across the pool table landing the point six. Joey Long and K-Dolla

stepped over and showed him some love. The Bread-Man seemed to smile the hardest when he saw Billy. *"And here's my son, Billy Gunz."* He shook his hand and gave him a hug.

"What up, pops?"

"Not much, just lining my pockets. I bet these cats must think these dice are loaded like a pistol from the way I'm sticking their asses up for their little money." Billy chuckled along with him. The Bread-Man handed Billy the dice. *"You shoot this one for me kid."* Billy shot the dice out his hand hoping for a six but crapped out with a seven.

"About time! The first break he done had from the dice all night." One of the gamblers around the table said as he picked up the dice.

The Bread-Man had lost ten stacks on that shoot and it didn't even fade him. Billy introduced me to him. I could tell he wasn't too fond of me. I tried to shake his hand he looked at then kept talking to Billy like I wasn't even there. *"Didn't I tell you the day you introduced me to K-Dolla not to bring any new people around me?"*

"I know but I thought this could be an exception because it's my brother." The Bread-Man pulled Billy to the side and put his hand on his shoulder.

"There are no exceptions. I don't care if it was yo mama, I don't want any new mothafuckas around me. The less I'm known the better. Who you put on your team is on you. That's your household. But you need to keep your circle small because when things go wrong, you'll know who to point your gun at. You dig where I'm coming from?"

"Yeah, pops, I get you." He squeezed Billy's shoulder.

"Good because I never want you to learn a lesson in this game the hard way. Dig, they gon' have some strippers here in a minute,

y'all stick around and enjoy yourselves. Me and Missy gonna split."

"Alright pops." I watched the Bread-Man and Missy leave out and all I could think was how that arrogant bastard was going to be a problem for me. He was going to try and separate me and Billy from each other. The nigga had my little brother calling him pops as if he ever needed a father figure in his life. He had me to look up to.

I can't lie, the whole thing kind of fucking with my head. Mostly because before I went to the joint Billy, Joey, and Missy all leaned on me for leadership. And now that Billy was the Bread-Man's right-hand man, everyone was taking orders from Billy, including me. The shit was embarrassing to me. I had to find a way to take back leadership.

I tried to get Billy to tell me about The Bread-Man's operation, but he stayed tight-lipped about it. I didn't let that dissuade me. I did a little ass-kissing and played the role of the perfect big brother. After several months Billy's lips began to loosen a bit. He told me about this Columbian name Carlito who the Bread-Man was getting his work from. He also told me that on the next meeting with Carlito the Bread-Man was planning to pick up three times his normal re-up amount. I didn't know exactly how much that would be, but I knew it had to be a lot and I knew I had to have it.

It was a week before the next meet with Carlito. I had a plan already put together in my head. I just needed to get Billy on board with it. If I got Billy on board, I knew everyone else would follow, well everyone but Missy...

"That completes what I've got to say. Won't you ask your boy, Joey Long, what happened next? He can tell it way better than me." Pay Pay was anxious to hear the rest of the story. He didn't bother to wait for Martin to approach Joey Long. Pay Pay was closer anyway.

Joey Long growled when Pay Pay snatched the tape off his mouth taking a piece of skin off his lip.

"Aww, the poor baby got a boo-boo?" Joey Long mean mugged Victoria as he sucked the blood off his lip. Pay Pay stepped into his line of sight blocking his view of Victoria.

"The baton's been passed to you."

"You want to know about the past, shit that happened when we were younger than you are now. You don't want to do that. Don't let the past be a matter to you, Pay Pay. Look at how well your life is, look at how close we all are. We're family, man."

"Just like y'all were my father's family, right?" Joey Long turned his head.

"You really want to throw away all that we built together for some mistakes of the past?"

"My father didn't die by an accident, he was murdered. Seven gunshots. There's no mistake in that. Tell me the goddamn story!"

"I can't! I can't. You just going to have to forgive me or kill me, Pay Pay."

"Forgive you? Let me tell you what my father taught my mother to teach me about forgiveness. A man could only be forgiven if he respects you enough to confess his wrongs, and then with sorrow in his heart ask you for forgiveness. So, if you want my forgiveness, then confess!" Joey Long tilted his head to the ceiling and closed his eyes a moment then opened them and looked at Pay Pay.

"You going to have to kill me because of what I did. I'm too ashamed to admit."

"You fucking coward!" Cîroc ran up on Joey Long punching him three times in the face before Pay Pay pulled him off him.

"You deny me of this! You is a bitch ass nigga, Joey Long."

"Call me what you want, but I rather take a bullet to the head than to tell a man that I consider my little brother the part I played in the death of his father." Pay Pay didn't know what hurt the most, the fact that a close friend of his killed his father or the fact that he wasn't even man enough to tell him what happened.

"Try to find forgiveness in hell then, nigga." Pay Pay spit in his face then turned his back on him. "Cîroc, have your way with him."

"Gladly. A bullet to the head is too quick of a death shot for him. I'm going to make this nigga feel our pain." Cîroc pulled out Cowboy's switchblade and Joey Long's eyes filled with terror. Cîroc drove the blade in and out his gut splashing blood everywhere. Joey Long screamed in agony. Cîroc backed off of him. "Now bleed to death, you lil bitch." Joey Long's shirt was covered in his blood. He moaned and groaned he was in so much pain. He begged Cîroc to finish him off.

"No love, no mercy, nigga. You remember that? A coward dies a thousand deaths, Joey Long. Stew in your pain." Cîroc walked off from him. Joey Long sat there praying for death to come to take him out of his misery. But God must've sent him to voicemail because it didn't seem like the grim reaper was coming soon enough. As much as it hurt, he knew he got just what he deserved.

King Dream

Chapter 21

Martin now drew his attention to Billy Gunz. He pulled the tape off his mouth. "Billy Gunz. We saved the best for last. You ain't going to clam up like Joey did, are you?"

"And risk getting diced up by your little sushi chef over there? Nah, I'll pass on the shank party. But I'm going to tell the story because Pay Pay deserves to know the truth. Besides, I'm a man and not a coward. No offense Joey Long." Joey Long paid him no mind. He was busy trying to stay conscious and keep his mind off the pain. Billy Gunz felt Pay Pay's eyes staring him down. He could see he was aching to know the rest of the story.

"You sure you're ready to hear what I'm about to say, Pay Pay? Once this genie is out of the bottle there's no putting him back. This is bound to change our bond forever." Pay Pay parked a barstool in front of Billy Gunz and took a seat. He wanted Billy Gunz to look him in the eye and tell him what he'd done.

"I'm not afraid of change. Without change, there's no evolution. So, go ahead tell me this life-changing story, and stop stalling."

"Alright, as you wish." Billy Gunz sucked his gold teeth then began telling the story...

I was in the kitchen busting down a brick of some straight drop. I mean this shit was so good you'd have to put gloves on, or it would seep through your pores. Cutthroat had come into the kitchen and by the look on his face, you could tell something was on his mind. "What's going on Cut?"

"I can't really call it. Can we rap for a minute?"

"Fo' sho'. Gon' tell me what's going on in that big ass head of yours." Cutthroat grabbed a Dr. Pepper out of the refrigerator then took a seat at the table next to me. He cracked open his soda and took a sip. Then he talks about how we weren't playing the

game smart by not securing our future. He got into this whole what if this and that happen, and we don't have shit to fall back on. We both agreed we never wanted to go back to being broke. When he felt he had sparked concern within me he slipped his plan on me.

His plan was for us to rob Carlito when he got back to his yacht after the next meeting. He told me to make sure Missy didn't find out. He was afraid by her being so attached to the Bread-Man that she might notify him of what we had planned. He didn't trust K-Dolla either, but I told him I wasn't going to do it without him, so he gave in.

The funny thing was Cutthroat thought he was really gaming me. Behind all the ass-kissing he was doing, I knew he was secretly jealous of me and plotting to take lead. But little did he know me, Javier, and Joey Long had been scratching out a plan for months to hit Carlito and the Bread-Man. I had been feeding Cutthroat bits of information about Carlito and how our next re-up would be a major load because I needed him for my plan to work out perfectly. Like the all-brawn and no brains dummy he is, he took the bait. A one-track mind like his is always predictable.

Right before the meeting, Javier called my hotel room from the car phone and informed me K-Dolla had successfully killed Carlito. I had no doubt he would. I found out a long time ago he had a weakness for Victoria. That's why I told Javier to offer him that proposition.

The next step of the plan we met up at the abandoned warehouse by the docks. When we arrived, Missy was just pulling up in the bread truck with the Bread-Man in the car in front of her. Cutthroat was ducked low in the backseat of my car so no one would see him. If the Bread-Man saw him he would've known, it was a setup. Me, Joey Long, and K-Dolla got out of the car and headed for the warehouse. K-Dolla was all shook up and trying his hardest not to look like it. The Bread-Man reached the entrance at the exact time we did. He put his arm around me. "Son, we are going to make a hell of money once we flip this load. We might have to come back next time with three bread trucks." *I gave him one of my award-winning fake smiles.*

Javier along with Gordo and Pablo were standing in the center of the warehouse awaiting us. The Bread-Man had this curious look on his face. "Did Carlito go take a piss or something? Where is he?" *Javier stood there looking into a pocket mirror combing his mustache.*

"Carlito's dead."

"What?"

"Had his neck broken on the church altar."

"Who did it?"

"You say that like you don't know. Like you had nothing to do with it." *Javier whistled and the two men that carried the bags out to the truck came running in with their pistols drawn on us.*

"That's bullshit! You trying to set me up, mothafucka!" *The Bread-Man dropped his suitcase and took out his twin nickel-plated Desert Eagles and before you knew it everybody had their guns out.* "I told Carlito he shouldn't trust you. You fucking snake. Billy y'all kill these mothafuckas and let's get up out of here." *Javier looked at me.*

"Don't forget our deal Billy Gunz." *The Bread-Man turned to me and I could see his heart break.*

"What is he talking about Billy?" *Joey Long and I turned our guns on him. K-Dolla looked confused, he didn't know who to keep his gun trained on.*

"Billy G, what are we doing?" *The Bread-Man was shocked by our betrayal.*

"I treated y'all like y'all were my own flesh and blood and y'all turn on me like this? For what? For some paper that we can get together? I taught you loyalty over royalty. Where's your loyalty?"

"I'm sorry, Pops. But it's my time to be the man." For the first time since I was a small child, I felt tears racing down my face. The Bread-Man was a better father to me than my own father. The hurt look on his face damn near broke me to my knees. For a second I didn't think I could go through with it. Then the sound of gunshots broke me out of that moment of weakness.

Cutthroat had crept in and shot the two Columbians that loaded the truck. The Bread-Man popped off two shots hitting Gordo in the stomach. Then he took cover behind an old factory machine. Javier's men were shooting at us. Which was all a part of our plan. Javier needed his men dead so that when he got back to Columbia no one could contest the story he would tell. K-Dolla was hiding behind an industrial fan shaking like a scared bitch. I told him to go to the truck and tell Missy the Bread-Man said to get the fuck out of here and don't stop until she gets home. I covered him as he ran out the door. Cutthroat was firing shots at Javier. I told him I had Javier, but I needed him to get Pablo off my ass. Javier ran out the side door and I followed him. I caught up with him on the dock not far from Carlito's yacht. "You ready?"

"Yeah."

"Where you want it?"

"Right here." Javier tapped his left thigh. I raised my gun and shot him in his thigh. He winced in pain as I helped him to his boat. "I didn't get the money. You owe me half when you re-up. Don't forget."

"I won't." I raced back to the warehouse. Pablo was down and so was the Bread-Man. Joey Long, K-Dolla, and Cutthroat were standing over him. He had caught a gunshot to the hip and chest from Cutthroat.

"K-Dolla, your turn. None of us is going to leave here with clean hands." K-Dolla raised his .38 with shaking hands and his

154

eyes closed, he shot him in the shoulder and arm. The Bread-Man moaned. Joey Long raised his gun.

"After all that I've done for Joey, is there any love in your heart for me?"

"Nope, no love no mercy." He squeezed off two shots hitting him in the stomach.

"Your turn Billy. Finish him off, little bro." I was surprised he was still alive after six shots. I could tell he was dying though. His breathing was slowing. He made a gesture with his hand for me to come closer and I did. I got down on my knees and brought my ear to his mouth.

He told me, "Revenge will be mine and your death will be the worst." Then he spat a mouthful of blood in my face. I got up and shot him in the chest. His head fell to the side and he was dead. The next day I had to complete the last phase of the plan, get rid of Cutthroat's power-hungry ass. I stashed a brick of heroin and a hot pistol in his, then I notified the police...

"That's the end of the story." Pay Pay wanted to choke the life out of Billy Gunz and the rest of them. But he had more questions he needed answers to.

"Billy, you son of a bitch! You killed him? You all killed my father?" Missy cried out.

"You telling me that all this time you didn't know they were the ones who killed him, Missy?"

"No, I swear. They told me it was Carlito. And I've always been afraid of the Columbians finding out Billy killed Carlito to avenge daddy. I didn't even know daddy had kids." Missy looked as if her whole world had just crumbled.

Joey Long fell face forward onto the ground still attached to the barstool. Wild-Child sat the barstool back up and checked his pulse. "He's dead." The reaper finally had come for him. Pay Pay continued drilling Billy Gunz with questions.

"How could you betray him like that?"

"How could you betray Baby Red?"

"Don't compare apples with oranges. We both know that was different. You knew I was his son. How?"

"I followed the Bread-Man one day to your house. It didn't take long to put two and two together and realize you were his son."

"You sought me out and made me a part of the Order. Why?"

"Despite what you think, I loved the Bread-Man. What I did that day has been haunting me all my life. I sought you out to in some way try to make things right. I tested you out with Baby Red and King Nut to see if you really had what it takes to be in this game. You surpassed all my expectations. You are definitely the Bread-Man's son. Believe this or not, but my plan was to turn the Order over to you, its rightful owner."

"I got one more question. What happened to the briefcase of money he had? Did you steal that too?"

"I can answer that one," Martin had cut in. "The day of the meeting, I got a call from Victoria saying some bogus shit was going to go down at the meeting and Uncle Bobby's life was in danger. I drove from San Antonio to Corpus Christi as fast I could. But it was too late the drama had already unfolded and everyone alive was already gone. I saw Uncle Bobby laid out in a puddle of blood. I kneeled next to his body. I thought he was dead, but he wasn't. He was damn near there. He could barely move or talk but he managed to tell me his dying wishes. He told me where he hid the briefcase. Then he told me to use the money to take care of Bella and his child she was carrying. His last words were for the three of us to avenge his death."

"He told you to look after Cîroc and his mama and not me mine?"

"That's because y'all was already well-off, Pay Pay. Aunt Resa raised you like she had a humble income. The truth was Uncle

Bobby made sure you and Aunt Resa had enough money to never have to worry about a thing. Bella and Cîroc, on the other hand, needed more guidance. Bella came from a household full of drug addicts. With him out of the picture, he was afraid she would hit rock bottom and turn to drugs. Sadly, a few years after Cîroc was born that exactly what she did. I've taken care of them ever since. As you know, my side of the family is wealthy, so I was able to manage caring for them with ease. I took the money from the brief-case and invested in businesses for both of you along with stock shares in our family's oil companies. Y'all are set for life."

"You know the whole story now big bro. So, what do you want to do with these mothafuckas?"

"Cîroc, let my daughter go. She ain't got shit to do with this." Cîroc walked over and stood behind Pumpkin's chair. He leaned down and kissed her on the cheek, she jerked her head away from him.

"You're right, Cutthroat. I'm going to cut her loose." Cîroc took the box cutter and split open her jugular vein. "See, you ain't the only one that can be cutthroat. Pun intended." Cutthroat screamed and shouted murderous insults at him. Cîroc came Cutthroat's way. "Cuz, give us pop's twins for these two." Martin pulled out the other nickel-plated Desert Eagle and handed one to Cîroc and the other to Pay Pay. Pay Pay took aim at Billy Gunz and Cîroc at Cutthroat. Cîroc wasted no time releasing all seven shots into Cutthroat's face and body killing him.

Pay Pay lowered his gun. "What, you had a change of heart?"

"Nope. Missy come here." Missy came. Pay Pay gave her a gun. "If you truly love my father, then you know what you need to do."

"You trying to get my bitch to turn against me? That won't happen, will it Missy? I was your family before the Bread-Man." Missy pointed the gun at Billy Gunz with tears clouding her eyes. Without saying a word, she pulled the trigger. Nothing happened. She tried again and again and nothing. There were no bullets in the gun.

Pay Pay felt her feelings for the Bread-Man were genuine. But he needed to know if given the choice back then between her loyalty for the Bread-Man and her loyalty for Billy Gunz who would she had chosen. Only a moment like that could give him the answer he desired.

Pay Pay pushed Missy to the side. "So long Billy Gunz."

BOOM! BOOM!

One to the heart and one to the head, and Billy Gunz was just a memory. They poured liquor all over the club then set the whole place ablaze. Like the club, the life Pay Pay once knew was now just smoke and flames. And he was moving forward with the nightmares of his past behind him.

The End

Submission Guideline

Submit the first three chapters of your completed manuscript to ldpsubmissions@gmail.com, subject line: Your book's title. The manuscript must be in a .doc file and sent as an attachment. Document should be in Times New Roman, double spaced and in size 12 font. Also, provide your synopsis and full contact information. If sending multiple submissions, they must each be in a separate email.

Have a story but no way to send it electronically? You can still submit to LDP/Ca$h Presents. Send in the first three chapters, written or typed, of your completed manuscript to:

LDP: Submissions Dept
Po Box 944
Stockbridge, Ga 30281

DO NOT send original manuscript. Must be a duplicate.

Provide your synopsis and a cover letter containing your full contact information.

Thanks for considering LDP and Ca$h Presents.

Coming Soon from Lock Down Publications/Ca$h Presents

BOW DOWN TO MY GANGSTA

By **Ca$h**

TORN BETWEEN TWO

By **Coffee**

BLOOD OF A BOSS **VI**

SHADOWS OF THE GAME II

TRAP BASTARD II

By **Askari**

LOYAL TO THE GAME **IV**

By **T.J. & Jelissa**

IF LOVING YOU IS WRONG... **III**

By **Jelissa**

TRUE SAVAGE **VIII**

MIDNIGHT CARTEL IV

DOPE BOY MAGIC IV

CITY OF KINGZ III

By **Chris Green**

BLAST FOR ME **III**

A SAVAGE DOPEBOY III

CUTTHROAT MAFIA III

DUFFLE BAG CARTEL VI

HEARTLESS GOON VI

By **Ghost**

A HUSTLER'S DECEIT III

KILL ZONE **II**

BAE BELONGS TO ME III

A DOPE BOY'S QUEEN III

By **Aryanna**

COKE KINGS V

KING OF THE TRAP III

By **T.J. Edwards**

GORILLAZ IN THE BAY V

3X KRAZY III

De'Kari

THE STREETS ARE CALLING II

Duquie Wilson

KINGPIN KILLAZ IV

STREET KINGS III

PAID IN BLOOD III

CARTEL KILLAZ IV

DOPE GODS III

Hood Rich

SINS OF A HUSTLA II

ASAD

KINGZ OF THE GAME VI

Playa Ray

SLAUGHTER GANG IV

RUTHLESS HEART IV

By Willie Slaughter

FUK SHYT II

King Dream

By Blakk Diamond

TRAP QUEEN

RICH $AVAGE II

By Troublesome

YAYO V

GHOST MOB II

Stilloan Robinson

CREAM III

By Yolanda Moore

SON OF A DOPE FIEND III

HEAVEN GOT A GHETTO II

By Renta

FOREVER GANGSTA II

GLOCKS ON SATIN SHEETS III

By Adrian Dulan

LOYALTY AIN'T PROMISED III

By Keith Williams

THE PRICE YOU PAY FOR LOVE III

By Destiny Skai

I'M NOTHING WITHOUT HIS LOVE II

SINS OF A THUG II

TO THE THUG I LOVED BEFORE II

By Monet Dragun

LIFE OF A SAVAGE IV

MURDA SEASON IV

GANGLAND CARTEL IV

CHI'RAQ GANGSTAS IV

KILLERS ON ELM STREET IV

JACK BOYZ N DA BRONX III

A DOPEBOY'S DREAM II

By **Romell Tukes**

QUIET MONEY IV

EXTENDED CLIP III

THUG LIFE IV

By **Trai'Quan**

THE STREETS MADE ME III

By **Larry D. Wright**

IF YOU CROSS ME ONCE II

ANGEL III

By **Anthony Fields**

FRIEND OR FOE III

By **Mimi**

SAVAGE STORMS III

By **Meesha**

THE STREETS WILL NEVER CLOSE II

By **K'ajji**

IN THE ARM OF HIS BOSS

By **Jamila**

HARD AND RUTHLESS III

MOB TOWN 251 II

By Von Diesel

LEVELS TO THIS SHYT II

King Dream

By Ah'Million

MOB TIES III

By SayNoMore

THE LAST OF THE OGS III

Tranay Adams

FOR THE LOVE OF A BOSS II

By C. D. Blue

MOBBED UP II

By King Rio

BRED IN THE GAME II

By S. Allen

Available Now

RESTRAINING ORDER **I & II**

By **CA$H & Coffee**

LOVE KNOWS NO BOUNDARIES **I II & III**

By **Coffee**

RAISED AS A GOON I, II, III & IV

BRED BY THE SLUMS I, II, III

BLAST FOR ME I & II

ROTTEN TO THE CORE I II III

A BRONX TALE I, II, III

DUFFLE BAG CARTEL I II III IV V

HEARTLESS GOON I II III IV V

A SAVAGE DOPEBOY I II

DRUG LORDS I II III

CUTTHROAT MAFIA I II

By **Ghost**

LAY IT DOWN **I & II**

LAST OF A DYING BREED I II

BLOOD STAINS OF A SHOTTA I & II III

By **Jamaica**

LOYAL TO THE GAME I II III

LIFE OF SIN I, II III

By **TJ & Jelissa**

BLOODY COMMAS I & II

SKI MASK CARTEL I II & III

KING OF NEW YORK I II,III IV V

RISE TO POWER I II III

COKE KINGS I II III IV

BORN HEARTLESS I II III IV

KING OF THE TRAP I II

By **T.J. Edwards**

IF LOVING HIM IS WRONG…I & II

LOVE ME EVEN WHEN IT HURTS I II III

By **Jelissa**

WHEN THE STREETS CLAP BACK I & II III

THE HEART OF A SAVAGE I II III

King Dream

By **Jibril Williams**
A DISTINGUISHED THUG STOLE MY HEART I II & III
LOVE SHOULDN'T HURT I II III IV
RENEGADE BOYS I II III IV
PAID IN KARMA I II III
SAVAGE STORMS I II
By **Meesha**
A GANGSTER'S CODE I &, II III
A GANGSTER'S SYN I II III
THE SAVAGE LIFE I II III
CHAINED TO THE STREETS I II III
BLOOD ON THE MONEY I II III
By **J-Blunt**
PUSH IT TO THE LIMIT
By **Bre' Hayes**
BLOOD OF A BOSS **I, II, III, IV, V**
SHADOWS OF THE GAME
TRAP BASTARD
By **Askari**
THE STREETS BLEED MURDER **I, II & III**
THE HEART OF A GANGSTA I II& III
By **Jerry Jackson**
CUM FOR ME I II III IV V VI VII
An **LDP Erotica Collaboration**
BRIDE OF A HUSTLA **I II & II**
THE FETTI GIRLS **I, II& III**

CORRUPTED BY A GANGSTA I, II III, IV

BLINDED BY HIS LOVE

THE PRICE YOU PAY FOR LOVE I II

DOPE GIRL MAGIC I II III

By **Destiny Skai**

WHEN A GOOD GIRL GOES BAD

By **Adrienne**

THE COST OF LOYALTY I II III

By Kweli

A GANGSTER'S REVENGE **I II III & IV**

THE BOSS MAN'S DAUGHTERS I II III IV V

A SAVAGE LOVE **I & II**

BAE BELONGS TO ME I II

A HUSTLER'S DECEIT I, II, III

WHAT BAD BITCHES DO I, II, III

SOUL OF A MONSTER I II III

KILL ZONE

A DOPE BOY'S QUEEN I II

By **Aryanna**

A KINGPIN'S AMBITON

A KINGPIN'S AMBITION **II**

I MURDER FOR THE DOUGH

By **Ambitious**

TRUE SAVAGE I II III IV V VI VII

DOPE BOY MAGIC I, II, III

MIDNIGHT CARTEL I II III

King Dream

CITY OF KINGZ I II

By **Chris Green**

A DOPEBOY'S PRAYER

By **Eddie "Wolf" Lee**

THE KING CARTEL **I, II & III**

By **Frank Gresham**

THESE NIGGAS AIN'T LOYAL **I, II & III**

By **Nikki Tee**

GANGSTA SHYT **I II &III**

By **CATO**

THE ULTIMATE BETRAYAL

By **Phoenix**

BOSS'N UP **I , II & III**

By **Royal Nicole**

I LOVE YOU TO DEATH

By Destiny J

I RIDE FOR MY HITTA

I STILL RIDE FOR MY HITTA

By **Misty Holt**

LOVE & CHASIN' PAPER

By **Qay Crockett**

TO DIE IN VAIN

SINS OF A HUSTLA

By **ASAD**

BROOKLYN HUSTLAZ

By **Boogsy Morina**

BROOKLYN ON LOCK I & II

By **Sonovia**

GANGSTA CITY

By **Teddy Duke**

A DRUG KING AND HIS DIAMOND I & II III

A DOPEMAN'S RICHES

HER MAN, MINE'S TOO I, II

CASH MONEY HO'S

THE WIFEY I USED TO BE I II

By Nicole Goosby

TRAPHOUSE KING **I II & III**

KINGPIN KILLAZ I II III

STREET KINGS I II

PAID IN BLOOD **I II**

CARTEL KILLAZ I II III

DOPE GODS I II

By **Hood Rich**

LIPSTICK KILLAH **I, II, III**

CRIME OF PASSION I II & III

FRIEND OR FOE I II

By **Mimi**

STEADY MOBBN' **I, II, III**

THE STREETS STAINED MY SOUL I II

By **Marcellus Allen**

WHO SHOT YA **I, II, III**

SON OF A DOPE FIEND I II

HEAVEN GOT A GHETTO
Renta
GORILLAZ IN THE BAY **I II III IV**
TEARS OF A GANGSTA I II
3X KRAZY I II
DE'KARI
TRIGGADALE I II III
Elijah R. Freeman
GOD BLESS THE TRAPPERS I, II, III
THESE SCANDALOUS STREETS I, II, III
FEAR MY GANGSTA I, II, III IV, V
THESE STREETS DON'T LOVE NOBODY I, II
BURY ME A G I, II, III, IV, V
A GANGSTA'S EMPIRE I, II, III, IV
THE DOPEMAN'S BODYGAURD I II
THE REALEST KILLAZ I II III
THE LAST OF THE OGS I II
Tranay Adams
THE STREETS ARE CALLING
Duquie Wilson
MARRIED TO A BOSS... I II III
By Destiny Skai & Chris Green
KINGZ OF THE GAME I II III IV V
Playa Ray
SLAUGHTER GANG I II III
RUTHLESS HEART I II III

By Willie Slaughter

FUK SHYT

By Blakk Diamond

DON'T F#CK WITH MY HEART I II

By Linnea

ADDICTED TO THE DRAMA I II III

IN THE ARM OF HIS BOSS II

By Jamila

YAYO I II III IV

A SHOOTER'S AMBITION I II

BRED IN THE GAME

By S. Allen

TRAP GOD I II III

RICH $AVAGE

By Troublesome

FOREVER GANGSTA

GLOCKS ON SATIN SHEETS I II

By Adrian Dulan

TOE TAGZ I II III

LEVELS TO THIS SHYT

By Ah'Million

KINGPIN DREAMS I II III

By Paper Boi Rari

CONFESSIONS OF A GANGSTA I II III

By Nicholas Lock

I'M NOTHING WITHOUT HIS LOVE

King Dream

SINS OF A THUG

TO THE THUG I LOVED BEFORE

By Monet Dragun

CAUGHT UP IN THE LIFE I II III

By Robert Baptiste

NEW TO THE GAME I II III

MONEY, MURDER & MEMORIES I II III

By **Malik D. Rice**

LIFE OF A SAVAGE I II III

A GANGSTA'S QUR'AN I II III

MURDA SEASON I II III

GANGLAND CARTEL I II III

CHI'RAQ GANGSTAS I II III

KILLERS ON ELM STREET I II III

JACK BOYZ N DA BRONX I II

A DOPEBOY'S DREAM

By **Romell Tukes**

LOYALTY AIN'T PROMISED I II

By Keith Williams

QUIET MONEY I II III

THUG LIFE I II III

EXTENDED CLIP I II

By **Trai'Quan**

THE STREETS MADE ME I II

By **Larry D. Wright**

THE ULTIMATE SACRIFICE I, II, III, IV, V, VI

KHADIFI

IF YOU CROSS ME ONCE

ANGEL I II

IN THE BLINK OF AN EYE

By **Anthony Fields**

THE LIFE OF A HOOD STAR

By Ca$h & Rashia Wilson

THE STREETS WILL NEVER CLOSE

By K'ajji

CREAM I II

By Yolanda Moore

NIGHTMARES OF A HUSTLA I II III

By King Dream

CONCRETE KILLA I II

By Kingpen

HARD AND RUTHLESS I II

MOB TOWN 251

By Von Diesel

GHOST MOB II

Stilloan Robinson

MOB TIES I II

By SayNoMore

BODYMORE MURDERLAND I II III

By Delmont Player

FOR THE LOVE OF A BOSS

King Dream

By C. D. Blue

MOBBED UP

By King Rio

BOOKS BY LDP'S CEO, CA$H

TRUST IN NO MAN

TRUST IN NO MAN 2

TRUST IN NO MAN 3

BONDED BY BLOOD

SHORTY GOT A THUG

THUGS CRY

THUGS CRY 2

THUGS CRY 3

TRUST NO BITCH

TRUST NO BITCH 2

TRUST NO BITCH 3

TIL MY CASKET DROPS

RESTRAINING ORDER

RESTRAINING ORDER 2

IN LOVE WITH A CONVICT

LIFE OF A HOOD STAR

King Dream

CPSIA information can be obtained
at www.ICGtesting.com
Printed in the USA
LVHW081444211121
704028LV00011B/1245

9 781955 270366